Date A Live
Search Natsumi

"Yes! You get it!
You get me, Shido!"

Natsumi
The seventh Spirit

"Uh... Oh.
I think you're
super pretty."

Shido Itsuka
A high school student

"What exactly is the
meaning of this?"

Origami Tobiichi
Shido's classmate

"Hmph."

"I-impossible..."

Kotori Itsuka
Ratatoskr Commander

"Tr-trick or treat...!"

Yoshino
A Spirit

CONTENTS

08

Koushi Tachibana

Illustrated by
Tsunako

New York

Koushi Tachibana

Translation by Jocelyne Allen
Cover art by Tsunako

This book is a work of fiction. Names, characters, places, and incidents are the product of the author's imagination or are used fictitiously. Any resemblance to actual events, locales, or persons, living or dead, is coincidental.

DATE A LIVE Vol.8 SEARCH NATSUMI
©Koushi Tachibana, Tsunako 2013
First published in Japan in 2013 by KADOKAWA CORPORATION, Tokyo.
English translation rights arranged with KADOKAWA CORPORATION, Tokyo through
TUTTLE-MORI AGENCY, Inc., Tokyo.

English translation © 2023 by Yen Press, LLC

Yen On
150 West 30th Street, 19th Floor
New York, NY 10001

Visit us at yenpress.com
facebook.com/yenpress
twitter.com/yenpress
yenpress.tumblr.com
instagram.com/yenpress

First Yen On Edition: February 2023
Edited by Yen On Editorial: Leilah Labossiere, Ivan Liang
Designed by Yen Press Design: Andy Swist

Yen On is an imprint of Yen Press, LLC.
The Yen On name and logo are trademarks of Yen Press, LLC.

The publisher is not responsible for websites (or their content) that are not owned by the publisher.

Library of Congress Cataloging-in-Publication Data
Names: Tachibana, Koushi, 1986– author. | Tsunako, illustrator. | Allen, Jocelyne, 1974– translator.
Title: Date a live / Koushi Tachibana ; illustration by Tsunako ; translation by Jocelyne Allen.
Other titles: Dēto a raibu. English
Description: First Yen On edition. | New York, NY : Yen On, 2021–
Identifiers: LCCN 2020054696 | ISBN 9781975319915 (v. 1 ; trade paperback) |
    ISBN 9781975319939 (v. 2 ; trade paperback) | ISBN 9781975319953 (v. 3 ; trade paperback) |
    ISBN 9781975319977 (v. 4 ; trade paperback) | ISBN 9781975319991 (v. 5 ; trade paperback) |
    ISBN 9781975320010 (v. 6 ; trade paperback) | ISBN 9781975348298 (v. 7 ; trade paperback) |
    ISBN 9781975349943 (v. 8 ; trade paperback)
Subjects: GSAFD: Science fiction. | Fantasy fiction.
Classification: LCC PL876.A23 D4813 2021 | DDC 895.63/6—dc23
LC record available at https://lccn.loc.gov/2020054696

ISBNs: 978-1-9753-4994-3 (paperback)
       978-1-9753-4995-0 (ebook)

10 9 8 7 6 5 4 3 2 1

LSC-C

Printed in the United States of America

Spirit

A uniquely catastrophic creature existing in a parallel world. Cause of occurrence and reason for existence unknown. Creates a spacequake and inflicts serious damage on her surroundings whenever she appears in this world. A very powerful fighter.

Strategy No. 1

Annihilate with force. This approach is very difficult, since the Spirit is extremely powerful, as noted above.

Strategy No. 2

...Date her and make her all weak in the knees.

Search Natsumi

Spirit No. 7
Astral Dress—Witch Type
Weapon—Broom Type [Haniel]

Prologue
Doppelgänger

"Wha…" Shido stood stock-still on the school roof, stunned, as he stared at the boy in front of him.

The reason was simple. There was something odd about the way the boy looked.

That said, it wasn't as though his face was that of a hideous monster. He wasn't terrifying in any particular way. Anyone looking in from the outside would assume he was nothing more than your average, ordinary boy.

Hair long enough to get in his eyes, plain features. His physique was average, he was of average height, and the clothing he wore was the Raizen High School winter uniform. Nothing out of the ordinary—an utterly normal boy.

But Shido shuddered as a chill ran up his spine. He swallowed hard and narrowed his eyes. "You…What *are* you?"

"What am I? What are you talking about?" The boy shrugged, and the corners of his mouth slid up into an amiable smile.

"I'm Shido Itsuka. Can't you tell by looking at me?"

"…!" Shido couldn't help but frown at the bizarre situation.

The boy standing in front of him had the exact same face as he did.

From the top of his head to the tips of his toes, the boy was a perfect copy of what Shido saw in the mirror every morning.

The boy with Shido's face looked at him, bemused, and then let out a sigh. "You really don't know who I am?"

"...?!" Shido frowned once again.

The voice had changed. It no longer sounded like Shido, but instead this time it sounded like a girl. And not only that—he'd heard this voice before.

"No way," he said. "Natsumi?!"

"Heh heh!" The boy smirked. "Correct. You finally got it, hmm, Shido?"

"Wh-what's with this look?! Why would you—?" Shido started.

"You ask me why?" Natsumi cut him off, grimacing. "I told you, didn't I? No one gets to just walk away after learning my secret. Brace yourself. I'm gonna mess you up, pound you down, and throw you around!"

She gave him a venomous thumbs-down.

Chapter 1
Halloween

"Hee-hee-hee! Say, daaarling? You can come closer, you know? Come on nooow."

"Uh. So, umm, Miku."

"What is iiiit? Oh, right. I found this lovely little Italian place the other day. Do you have any plans toniiight? How about you join me?"

"Oh, uh, I have to make supper for Tohka and everyone, so…"

"Whaaat? Then let's go with Tohka and everyone, too. I'm not a petty woman, you knooooow. Of course, it would be my treat, so please don't worry about that."

"No, but seriously, Miku." Shido Itsuka looked at the girl snuggling up to him with an innocent smile on her face, a troubled look upon his own.

Bluish-purple hair, smooth and shiny like silk, and well cared-for, luminous skin. She was—without exaggeration—gorgeous.

Miku Izayoi was in the grade above Shido, but her behavior was always so childish that it was hard to believe she was actually the older one. Her body, however, was definitely mature. Every time she moved, her more-than-ample bosom pressed into Shido, leaving him at a loss for what to do. All he could do was look anywhere but at her, a cold sweat popping up on his forehead.

But it wasn't only Miku's innocent come-on that was making Shido freeze up.

"…"

Someone was glaring intensely at him.

His little sister Kotori was sitting right in front of them. Hair tied up in two black ribbons, eyes round like acorns, and a Chupa Chups stuck in her mouth. She wore a crimson jacket over her shoulders and was resting her chin in her hands as she grumpily watched Shido and Miku's (one-way) flirting.

They were in a room on the airship *Fraxinus*. The space was dim, as though the lights had been purposefully lowered. Chairs had been set out in the center of the room and long tables set up around them. The scene was like a stressful job interview or even an audience at court. Miku didn't seem to be bothered in the slightest by the tense atmosphere.

"Maybe that's enough for now, Miku," Kotori said, finally.

"Hmm? Whaaat do you ever mean?" Miku said, innocently.

"I. Told. You!" Kotori gritted her teeth and slammed a hand down on the table. "This is an inquiry! Shido's only here as a special favor, because *you* said you wouldn't do it unless your 'darling' came!"

"Ohhh, that's right." Miku laughed and turned toward Kotori. But her hand remained wrapped around Shido's arm.

Kotori sighed heavily as she flipped through the documents in front of her. "So then, let's get on with the questions."

"Yes, yes. Pleeease do," Miku said, warmly.

Kotori let out another sigh. "There are a number of things I want to ask you about your powers and your Angel. But I'll set those aside for now. First…" She snapped her index finger out at Miku as she said, "I need to ask about the being that made you a Spirit."

"…!"

Miku stiffened.

"You're not a natural-born Spirit—you were originally human," Kotori continued. "No mistake there, right?"

"…"

Miku frowned slightly and looked pained. She started breathing a little faster.

Shido wondered for a second if there was something preventing

Miku from answering Kotori's question, but then he remembered that she had become a Spirit at a time when she had lost her faith in human beings entirely and saw no good in the world. She was probably just reluctant to speak of that time.

"Are you all right, Miku?" he asked. "If this is difficult for you, we can take a break."

"No, it's all right." Miku shook her head. "I have you now, daaaarling. I've decided to move forward, and that means parting with everything in the past, too."

"Miku." He patted her back gently in encouragement.

"Yes, that's right," Miku said. "Several months ago...everyone in my life betrayed me. I lost my voice due to psychological aphonia, and with it, all hope. That's when God appeared before me."

Kotori's gaze sharpened the tiniest bit. Shido furrowed his brow, slightly.

But Miku appeared not to notice this as she continued speaking. "'Don't you want power? More power than you've ever imagined, enough to change the whole world,' God said and handed me this shining purple jewel. I reached out to take it, and the jewel melted into my body. And then I had the magical voiiice that could make anyone do whatever I told them to."

"I see," Kotori said, a complicated look on her face, and flicked up the stick of the Chupa Chups in her mouth. "Tell me everything you know about this 'God' of yours."

"Everything? Ooh." Miku's eyebrows climbed up her forehead. "It felt strange somehooow. They were definitely there, but I couldn't really see them. It was like they were covered in static. And I could hear their voice and understand what they were saying, but I had no idea what their voice sounded like. Pixelated and blurred out, like on TV."

"Oh," Kotori said, with a sigh. But she didn't look that dejected. She had most likely anticipated this response. "Okay, next question. After you gained your Spirit powers, were you ever overcome with destructive urges? Did you ever feel your sense of self erode?"

"Destructive...urges? No, nothing in particular comes to mind."

"Hmm." Scowling, Kotori made some notes on the page in front of her.

"Kotori, are you maybe...?" Shido asked.

"Yes." Kotori nodded. "I thought maybe the same things that happened in my case might have happened with Miku as well. But that does make me wonder. Is the difference because of the nature of the Spirit power? Or is it a matter of individual aptitude? Or could it be that Phantom used me to figure out the trick of giving a human Spirit powers? Ha! If that's the case, though, I really hate the idea of being used as an experiment," she said, bitterly, and shrugged.

Shido gritted his teeth and clenched his fists.

Phantom. The being that had given Miku and Kotori powers and changed them into Spirits. Was this mysterious entity a Spirit? A human being? Something else entirely? Why could they turn people into Spirits? And for what purpose? They were shrouded in mystery, a literal phantom.

"Mmph."

Shido let his thoughts race, and then felt an abrupt tug on his arm. He looked up and saw Miku sulking and puffing her cheeks out.

"Could both of you pleeease not ignore me and just sit there thinking," she begged.

"Oh. Sorry." Shido smiled at her.

"I'm sorry." Kotori cleared her throat. "But don't worry. The inquiry's only just begun. I'm going to be listening very closely to everything you have to say. We can't discard the possibility that your memories were manipulated by Phantom, though, so we're going to put a few electrodes on your head to watch your brain waves, okay?"

Kotori grinned, while Miku looked apprehensive.

The sun was setting by the time Kotori finally let Miku go.

After being transferred to just outside the Itsuka house via the *Fraxinus* transporter, Miku staggered in exhaustion and leaned against Shido.

"H-hey, whoa!" he cried. "You okay?"

"I-I'm so tiiiired." Miku exhaled, heavily. "Honestly, all I want to do today is go straight home and dive into my futon. Darling, I am so sorry, but can we go to that restaurant another time?"

"Huh? Oh, sure, that's fine," Shido said.

Miku clasped her hands in front of her chest, her face brightening dramatically. "Mm! Oh you! You really are so kiiind, darling!" And then she snuggled up against him even more.

"H-hey, isn't this sort of thing kind of dicey for an idol?" Shido averted his eyes, his face red, and Miku looked at him, blankly.

Yes. The girl innocently embracing Shido, Miku Izayoi, was a famous idol with a miraculous singing voice. Because she had long hidden her identity, her face hadn't been particularly well-known. But she'd lifted her ban on TV appearances the previous month, and now her face was recognized across the country. Anyone who caught her in a defenseless moment like this would snap a scandalous photo.

But the corners of Miku's mouth turned up neatly, as if she'd read his mind. "Hee hee! It's fiiine. This is nothing. If the paparazzi are hiding around here, I'll pose for them nicely and flash them a peace sign. They can come at me Friday, Sunday, whenever they want."

"Oh, I think Sunday'll be all right, though." Shido smiled, dryly.

Miku giggled. "Darling, you said even if no one else will listen to my songs, you'll always be my fan, riiiight? So it's all good. As long as I have you, I don't care what happens."

"Oh, right, I guess." Shido bowed his head a bit bashfully.

A grin spread across Miku's face as she pulled away from him. "Then I'll be heading home for today. I'll be waiting with bated breath until I can see you again, darling."

"Yeah, see you."

"Well then." Miku wound her arms around Shido's neck and pushed her lips forward.

"Wha—?! Wh-wh-wh-what are you doing?!" he cried.

"Hmm? What?" She raised an eyebrow. "A goodbye kiss, of course."

"I-I mean, I know you're not worried about a scandal, but this is too much," he protested.

"Mmm, honestly, you're so shyyyy. It's fine. Come on." Miku tightened her arms around his neck, and his face was inextricably pulled toward hers.

"H-hey, hang on!" he yelped.

"Ah! What are you two doing?!" a voice shouted from one side.

Shido and Miku simultaneously turned toward the voice and found a girl standing there, eyes wide open, hands trembling.

Hair the color of a night sky spilling over her shoulders down her back, and beautiful crystalline eyes. An absolute beauty, the sort you could never forget after seeing her just once.

Tohka Yatogami. Shido's classmate and neighbor. And like Miku, she was a Spirit whose powers Shido had locked away. She had come to the Itsuka house because it was almost time for supper.

"T-Tohka!" he stammered.

"Oh my, Tohka! I haven't seen you in aaages," Miku said, cheerfully.

Tohka stomped over and yanked Shido and Miku apart. And then as if to protect Shido, she threw her arms out and stood between the two of them.

"You're not hurt, are you, Shido?" Tohka narrowed her eyes into a sharp glare. "I heard Miku here had changed her ways. What was that, though?!"

Shido then heard more footsteps march in from the direction Tohka had come.

"Hmph, quite the nerve to attempt to get your claws into Shido, the shared property of Yuzuru and myself. Good! We shall school you thoroughly in the mighty fearsomeness of the Yamais!"

"Warning. In the event of touching Shido, please submit a request to that effect to those who hold ownership, Yuzuru and Kaguya."

The identical twins turned toward Miku and dropped into fighting stances.

Kaguya, hair pulled back and determined look on her face, and

Yuzuru, braided hair and blank expression. From the neck up, the only ways to tell them apart were their hairstyles and their facial expressions. Drop your eyes below the neck, however, and you would find an obvious physical difference.

"I-I think. We're not supposed to stand…in the middle of the road…," a small girl with her hat pulled down over her eyes—Yoshino—said, her cheeks reddening.

The rabbit puppet on her left hand—Yoshinon—flapped its mouth open and closed. *"Right? Not good at all. Yoshino hasn't had her chance to try the goodbye kiss yet. No going and stealing him out from under her!"*

"Y-Yoshinon…?" Yoshino hurriedly covered the puppet's mouth, and it flailed its arms, like it was struggling for air.

Yoshino had been moved to the apartment building next door a few days earlier after living in the isolation space on *Fraxinus*, so that she could gradually get used to living a regular life.

Just like Tohka, the Yamai sisters and Yoshino were also Spirits and had a serious history with Miku. She had taken control of all three of them, body and mind, when she made her Angel manifest the previous month. Maybe because of that, they were still slightly on guard against her.

But Miku was oblivious to this. Her eyes lit up when she saw the three Spirits.

"Goodness! It's been so long. Yoshino, Kaguya, Yuzuru—I'm so sorry about that whole thiiiing last month. I've been wanting to apologize to you." She bowed neatly.

Confused, the girls looked at each other, awkwardly.

But this apology didn't reassure Tohka. She continued to stand between Miku and Shido. "What are you up to? You were trying to do something to Shido just now!"

"Hmm?" Miku arched an eyebrow. "It was a goodbye kiss? Don't you aaaalways give him one, Tohka?"

"G-goodbye…kiss?" Tohka frowned, dubiously, and looked back at Shido. "Is that something we're supposed to do?"

He shook his head, vigorously. He couldn't let her get the wrong idea. "Th-that's a lie! I mean a kiss when you say goodbye, that's just—"

"Whaaat? It's wonderful, though?" Miku said. "Why don't you try it, too, Tooohka?"

"Wha—?!"

Shido, Tohka, and even Yoshino and the Yamai sisters all gasped.

But Miku stared at them, puzzled, as if their reaction was the surprising thing here, and then clapped her hands like she had just remembered something.

"Oh, yes! I had a delightful idea. First, I'll kiss Daaaarling. And then I will kiss you, Tohka. What do you think? Two birds with one stone! Isn't it revolutionaryyy?"

"Wh-why do I have to kiss *you*?!"

"Hmm? It's just, I'll have kissed my darling right before that, yes?"

"Mm. Right."

"So thaaaat means, it would be like you were kissing him, too, Tohka."

"Hmm… I-I get it…" Tohka paused, thoughtfully.

"Hey, whoa!" Shido interjected. "Don't just start agreeing with her!"

Tohka shuddered. "Y-you dirty Miku! Trying to trick me!"

"I would never," Miku said. "Oh! So then, how about we do this? First, you and I kiss, and then I'll kiss Darling. I'll make sure to make him feeeel your passion."

"Wha…?!" Tohka's jaw dropped.

"Hmm." Miku clasped her hands at her chest as though offering up a prayer, lowered her eyes, and pushed her lips toward Tohka.

Tohka shook her head in a panic and fled.

"Aaah, why are you running awaaay?" Miku frowned. "Please come back!"

"St-stay away from me!" Tohka half-screamed, running toward Yoshino and the sisters.

"Eek!"

"F-fool! Come not this way!"

"Shiver. We should flee, Kaguya."

They all ran from Miku.

"Aah! Well, if that's how it iiiis, then I'll leave you all to take care of each other!"

""""Aaaaaaaaah!""""

"Ha. Ha-ha…" Shido watched a thoroughly delighted Miku chase after the others and laughed weakly.

He felt like this went beyond antagonism or payback for interrupting their kiss or anything like that. It was more like she was simply trying to open herself up to the others.

After returning Shido and Miku to the ground, Kotori sat in her office on *Fraxinus*, looking thoughtful as she went over Miku's testimony. "Hmm."

On the screen before her was a transcription of Miku's recorded voice. Kotori cross-referenced this as she prepared a report to submit to the Rounds. Normally, she would leave this type of work to someone else in the organization. But when it came to the mysterious Phantom, Kotori felt like she needed to handle it herself, given that she had faced Phantom directly.

Miku was the only person Kotori knew, besides Shido and herself, who had encountered the elusive being. Her testimony could very well contain information that might lead them to Phantom's true identity, so Kotori couldn't delegate this job to anyone else.

"The purple Sefirah Phantom gave Miku," she muttered to herself as she tapped at her console, following the text with her eyes. "I wonder how many Sefirah they have. What if they can make an inexhaustible supply…?"

And then she felt something cold pressed against her cheek and let out a shriek. "Eep?!"

She yanked her face up in surprise and caught sight of a girl around the same age as her holding out a can of coffee. Her hair was tied back in a ponytail, and there was a beauty mark under her left eye. She looked a little like Shido somehow.

"All fine and good to be passionate about your work, but aren't you overdoing it a bit?" the girl—Mana Takamiya—said with a grin.

"You're one to talk," Kotori retorted, indignantly, and accepted the chilled can. She cracked it open, took a swig of the liquid inside, and a bitter, adult taste spread across her tongue.

"So? What's going on?" Mana asked. "Any developments?"

"Unfortunately, no. All I know is that the Phantom we saw five years ago and this 'something' that reached out to Miku are most likely the same—" Kotori's eyebrow twitched up, and she cut herself off. "How are you here anyway?"

"Huh?" Mana cocked her head curiously. "How? I came in through the door like normal. See? Not even noticing that, that's proof you're exhausted. You need to—"

"Not that!" Kotori shouted and slammed a fist down on her desk. "You were told to rest! You were ripped to pieces out there after your reckless actions!"

Although Mana Takamiya was currently under the protection of Ratatoskr, she was formerly a Wizard with the second enforcement division at DEM Industries. During her time there, she had undergone magical processing in all parts of her body, and while this had given her tremendous power, she paid a steep price for it, physically.

"I told you, didn't I?" Kotori said. "If we use Ratatoskr's specialized facilities to treat you immediately, we might be able to extend your lifespan a little at least! And yet here you are!"

"A-ah, well, that is true. Mm-hmm. H-ha ha-ha! Woh-kay, I should get going." Mana smiled sheepishly and started to back away.

Kotori stood up from her chair and prevented Mana from retreating. To put it more plainly, she wrapped her arms around the other girl tightly and pressed her face to her back.

"K-Kotori?" Mana said, bewildered.

"Thanks," Kotori said, quietly. "If you hadn't been on *Fraxinus* that time, I don't know what would have happened."

"..."

Mana looked back at the other girl without saying anything, then gently patted Kotori's head. "We're in the same boat there. I mean, you saved me. I'm actually relieved that I could pay that debt back so soon."

Kotori wiped away the tears that had welled up in her eyes and shrugged with a chuckle. "I dunno. It's like, you really *are* Shido's little sister. I'm kinda jealous."

"Huh?"

"It's nothing. But..." Kotori knitted her brow and tightened her grip around Mana to hold her fast. "I'm grateful for what you did. But this and that are two separate stories. You're going to go to our facilities and get the treatment you need."

"O-oh, but look," Mana protested. "I have to go after Nightmare. No one else can."

"The Kurumi investigation is urgent, it's true," Kotori agreed. "But your body just can't take any more!"

"Uh. Umm. Kotori? Your cute face is becoming entirely frightening." Mana pulled away, a tense smile on her face, and Kotori squeezed even harder to keep her from escaping.

"Commander Itsuka." A window popped up on Kotori's screen and a voice came from the speakers. *"We're receiving a message from head offi—?!"*

Shiizaki, the *Fraxinus* crew member in the window, gasped and shuddered. Almost as if she were looking at something she wasn't supposed to be seeing.

"Ah!" Kotori cried. Just like she could see Shiizaki, Shiizaki could also see her. And at that moment, Kotori appeared to be passionately embracing Mana. A scene like this practically begged to be misunderstood.

Kotori hurriedly released Mana and turned toward the screen.

"Don't get the wrong idea! I just grabbed onto Mana because she was trying to—"

"Okay. I'll throw myself into pursuing Nightmare! I'll follow up later with my results!" Freed from Kotori's restraint, Mana scampered away.

Kotori reached out to grab her collar, but it was too late. Mana slipped past her fingertips and out of the office.

"Ah! You!" Kotori shouted. "You're getting that treatment when you get back!"

"I'll think about it!" Mana said, with a wave.

The automatic door of the office closed with a *chk*.

"Honestly. That girl." Kotori scratched her head, sat down, and turned toward the screen. "So. What? Head office?"

"Oh! Y-yes. Control's on the private line. Should I connect you?"

"Yes. Please do."

"Roger that." Shiizaki tapped at her console, and she disappeared from the screen, replaced by someone new.

This was a face Kotori had seen many times, one of the secretaries of Elliot Woodman, the chair of the Ratatoskr Rounds.

"I apologize for the interruption, Commander Itsuka. I know you're busy."

"That's fine. What is it?"

"Er, the truth is that Lord Woodman..." the secretary continued speaking, looking slightly awkward.

Sunday, October 15.

The city was decorated in full Halloween mode. Shido and Tohka walked toward the shopping district to pick up groceries for supper.

"Oohh. Shido. What's that?" Tohka pointed at an enormous pumpkin monster adorning a storefront.

"Oh, that's a jack-o'-lantern," he told her. "You make them by carving up pumpkins. That one's not a real pumpkin, though. It's plastic."

"Pumpkin?" Tohka frowned. "That monster's orange, though? Aren't pumpkins green?"

"Yeah, in Japan, they're mostly green," he agreed. "But I guess they have pumpkins like that in other countries."

"It's just…so big. You could make a stew and tempura and soup and *still* have some left," Tohka said, admiringly, her eyes wide, as she nodded in agreement with herself.

He'd actually heard that the type of pumpkin used for jack-o'-lanterns was basically for looks only and not really eaten, but…there was no real need to crush Tohka's dreams.

"Hmm," he said. "Okay, since they're in season, how about we get pumpkin for supper today? I'm pretty sure I've got some ground beef left. I could do a stew or croquettes."

"Ooh!" Tohka waved her hand vigorously, eyes shining. "Mm, that's really great! I know what stew is, but croquettes? I thought you made those with potatoes?"

"Normally, yeah. But if you make them with pumpkin, they're sweet and very tasty."

Tohka closed her eyes for several seconds, as if imagining the flavor, and then swallowed her drool. "Mm. Let's have croquettes today! It's decided, so let's go, Shido!"

"Oh, hey! You have to watch where you're—" Shido started to warn her, but it was too late.

Tohka slammed into someone coming around the corner and was knocked backward onto her butt. "Ngh!"

"Whoops," the person said.

"Oh, come on." Shido rolled his eyes. "I *just* warned you. Are you okay?"

"Mm… Mm-hmm."

After helping Tohka up, Shido turned toward the person she'd just run into and found a foreign man in his fifties in a wheelchair with a spectacled woman in her mid-twenties pushing it.

"I'm sorry," Shido said. "We weren't watching where we were going. Are you hurt? Hey, Tohka, you have to apologize too."

"Umm. Sorry. I wasn't looking." Tohka bowed, apologetically.

The man shook his head with a gentle smile and spoke in surprisingly fluent Japanese. "No, we're sorry. Are you all right, miss?"

"Mm." Tohka nodded. "No injuries."

"That's a relief. If I were to hurt a lovely young woman such as yourself, I would have to go straight to hell," the man joked. To be able to produce such a line so smoothly, the man had no doubt been quite the playboy in the past.

Shido secretly noted that he could learn a thing or two. Although the young lady in question was not reddening in the cheeks, but rather staring blankly.

The man clapped his hands, as if he'd just remembered something. "I did want to ask you something, though. Do you know where the municipal hospital is?"

"Hospital?" Shido said. "Oh, you'll want to go straight up this street full of shops, and when you come out onto a road, turn left. Then make a right at the third intersection, go straight and then you'll see it."

The man shook his head.

"I don't really understand," he said. "I'm sorry. Would you mind showing us the way?"

Shido scratched at his cheek, awkwardly. They were supposed to get groceries. Then again, the hospital wasn't that far away. He supposed it wouldn't take too long.

"Sure thing. It's this way," he said, and started up the shopping street.

"Sorry for the bother," the man said. "Japanese people really are so nice. I appreciate it."

"Not at all, it's nothing," Shido replied. "Mr....umm."

"Oh, please call me Baldwin. And this is Karen." The man—Baldwin—pointed to the woman pushing his wheelchair.

"Hello," Karen said, simply, before falling silent once more. Pale Nordic blond hair, blue eyes. Even though Shido had definitely never met her before, for some reason, he got the feeling that he'd seen her elsewhere.

"Is something wrong?" Baldwin asked.

"Oh. No," he said, hurriedly. "I'm Shido Itsuka."

"Tohka Yatogami," Tohka said.

Baldwin nodded, looking pleased. "Mm-hmm. I must give thanks to God that I was able to meet such a wonderful couple in this unfamiliar place."

"Pft!" Shido sputtered.

"Mm...?" Tohka tilted her head, perhaps not understanding the meaning of Baldwin's words, or maybe wondering at Shido's reaction.

"Are you all right, Shido?" Baldwin asked, concerned.

"W-we're not actually a couple," Shido stammered.

"Oh-ho! My mistake then. Apologies." Baldwin shrugged, and Shido wiped away the perspiration from his forehead.

But Tohka was poking a finger into his back. "Shido. What's a couple?"

"Huh?! Oh, the thing there is, uh…"

When Shido was at a loss, Baldwin turned amused eyes on Tohka.

"Tohka. How long has it been since you met Shido?"

"Huh? Hmm." She thought for a second. "About six months, I guess."

"I see," Baldwin said. "So that would make it April then. That's right around the time of school entrance ceremonies and the start of lessons, yes? Is that where you met?"

"No. I met Shido during a spacequake—"

"Aaah!" Shido cried out to cut off Tohka's overly honest response.

It was only now Tohka realized the issue. Her eyes flew open, and she continued, trying to cover up the gaffe. "N-not that. A spacequake's a spacequake, but you know, it wasn't like I caused it. I mean…"

"W-we met in the shelter during a spacequake!" Shido said.

"Mm-hmm! That!" Tohka bobbed her head up and down in agreement.

It was a bit awkward, but well, it would work as an answer to the question. Shido timidly turned his eyes toward Baldwin.

The man was simply watching the two of them go back and forth with a smile and not a trace of suspicion on his face. They had apparently covered Tohka's slip well enough. Shido let out a sigh of relief.

But there was something there, in the look on Baldwin's face that made Shido uncomfortable, like the older man had actually figured their entire situation out.

"You did? That's fate for you." Baldwin exhaled slowly and with real emotion. "Tohka. Are you happy now?"

"Hmm?" Her eyes widened at the sudden question. But that was the extent of her doubt. She nodded, deeply. "Mm-hmm. I'm very happy!"

"You are?" Baldwin smiled, kindly.

And then a shrill siren began to blare from speakers all over the shopping street.

Vwnnnnnnnnnnnnnnnnnnnnnnnnmmmmm.

"The alarm!" Shido shouted, while an announcement urging everyone to evacuate began to play, and shoppers hurriedly headed for the nearest shelter.

But he couldn't evacuate to the shelters with everyone else. The spacequake alarm also meant the appearance of a Spirit. He had to contact *Fraxinus* immediately and get them to pick him up with the transporter.

"Uh! Umm! Mr. Baldwin!" he said, panicking. "It's dangerous here. Please evacuate right away!"

"I will do just that. And you?"

"Huh? I-I just have a thing to do, so," Shido stammered.

"Aah, that was a mean question, wasn't it?" Baldwin smiled and shrugged. "I'll pray that we are able to meet again someday. Good luck. Take care of that Spirit."

"Huh?" Shido furrowed his brow.

But Baldwin said nothing in reply, instead giving an order to Karen and returning the way they had come.

"Shido, what are you doing?" Tohka said.

"R-right." Shido took his eyes off of Baldwin and Karen as he pulled the earpiece he used to communicate with *Fraxinus* out of his pocket.

*   *   *

"What shall you do now? Commander Itsuka has called a number of times," Karen said, as soon as they left Shido Itsuka and Tohka Yatogami, while she pushed the wheelchair forward.

Baldwin glanced at her. "Ha-ha! I suppose I've worried her. Still, with the spacequake, *Fraxinus* will be busy. We'll be good and evacuate for now. Oh, and there was that DEM employee caught during the Berserk incident. Since we're in Japan anyway, perhaps we could have a little chat with him."

"Understood. I'll make the arrangements," Karen said in a business-like tone.

Baldwin nodded. "So? Anything unusual with them?"

"As far as I can see, no issue at the moment," she replied. "They're extremely stable."

"They are? That's good news," he said, and sighed.

Last month, the boy Shido Itsuka had manifested multiple Angels against an "inverted" Spirit. Naturally, Baldwin had received a report on the results of the investigation into this incident, but he felt like he couldn't be completely free of concern until he met the boy himself.

But his fears appeared to have been unwarranted. He recalled the bounce in Tohka's voice, and the corners of his mouth curled up.

"I'm glad we came to Japan. She really did seem happy." Elliot Baldwin Woodman smiled.

◇

"This is... I dunno... kinda creepy." After being transferred from *Fraxinus* to the location of the spacequake, Shido looked out at the scene around him, a bead of sweat trickling down the side of his face.

A vast circle two kilometers across had been gouged out of the ground, like the soil had been neatly prepared for some new endeavor. The mark of a spacequake, the spontaneous natural disaster that had been deemed a shaking of space itself.

But Shido wasn't looking at these traces of the catastrophe. He was focused on the south side of the area lost to the spacequake. The structures there seemed oddly out of place in the city.

The rails of a rollercoaster cut off in midair, a merry-go-round missing the horse heads. Cracked coffee cups, a half-destroyed house of mirrors. They were all rusted and covered in moss, making it doubtful that the spacequake was the cause of the damage.

The transporter had sent Shido to the remains of an amusement park on the outskirts of Tengu. He didn't know its actual name. Neighboring residents only ever called it "Monster Land." Apparently, by some stroke of luck, the facility had just narrowly escaped the Great Southern Kanto Spacequake thirty years earlier, but of course, the number of visitors declined after the disaster. After receiving practically no customers, the amusement park was forced to shut down.

On top of that, because it hadn't actually been damaged in the spacequake, the park wasn't allocated any of the subsidies for redevelopment, and had fallen into ruin, while other facilities sprang up one after the other all over the city.

The circle of damage from the current spacequake also just barely overlapped with the park premises so that the rusted attractions remained as they had been.

Given that it was also dusk, the entire effect was distinctly creepy. It was like the haunted house, nothing more than a side show in the amusement park's original incarnation, had eaten away at the entire place and expanded its territory.

"This is a bit *too* atmospheric," Shido muttered, grimacing.

"*Quit complaining.*" Kotori's voice came through the earpiece in his right ear. "*The Spirit's already moving west from the spacequake's epicenter. The AST'll be arriving soon enough. Make contact before they add their fun to the mix.*"

"Roger!" Shido said, and headed south—toward the deserted amusement park.

To be honest, he would rather not have, but he didn't have the luxury of saying no. Although they had gotten the jump this time, the

AST—Anti-Spirit Team—would be on their way in no time at all. He had to talk with the Spirit for at least a couple of minutes before they got there.

But his feet abruptly stopped. "Huh?" He gaped, rooted to the spot.

"Hey? What are you doing? The Spirit's signal's further—" Kotori started, and then she too stopped. Most likely because she'd caught sight of what Shido was looking at via the autonomous cameras.

At a certain point, the ruins of the amusement park gave way to a gaudy, tasteless area of deformed gothic buildings and crosses marking graves.

"Wh-what is this?" He got the curious sensation that he'd wandered into a horror comedy produced with the latest CG or a Visual Kei music video, and unconsciously pinched his cheek. Naturally, all that did was make him feel a sharp pain. "The park attraction's changing? ...No, it can't be, right?"

"Hold on. It's very faint, but there's a Spirit signal in the area," Kotori said, having apparently regained her composure. *"I don't know the details, but this is most likely connected with the Spirit's abilities."*

Shido swallowed hard as he stared at the abnormal landscape spreading out ahead of him.

"Ooooh?"

He heard a voice from above and jerked his face up.

On the roof of the church towering before him, he caught sight of a strange silhouette. A woman sat atop the cross on the church's gable and behind her glowed the orange of the evening sun. Because she was backlit, he couldn't make out her face, but the distinctive hat she wore was clear as day.

Wide brim, cone bent at the tip. The sort of thing a fairytale witch wore.

"Hee-hee-hee! I never meet humans other than the AST when I'm *pulled* to this side." The Spirit giggled and jumped down from the cross, floating lightly through the air to land in front of Shido.

A tall woman clad in an Astral Dress the color of the setting sun and the black of the night sky. Based on her looks, he'd guess she was maybe a little over twenty years old. Slender limbs, ample bosom. Perfect proportions to put a pin-up model to shame.

She was beautiful, like she had been built to specification, to create the ideal woman. Long shiny hair fell from under the brim of the wide hat, and eyes like emeralds peered out through the gaps to stare at Shido with great interest.

"Hmmm?" The Spirit leaned in as though assessing Shido's worth.

Caught off guard, Shido unconsciously jumped.

The Spirit giggled again as if amused by his reaction.

"Uh. Umm. I'm—" Shido started.

"Huh." The Spirit reached out a hand to nudge Shido's chin up. "You're pretty cute, aren't you? What's up, hmm? I thought an alarm went off in this world when I appeared?"

"Th-that's..." Completely knocked off balance, Shido fumbled for the words, and then heard Kotori's voice in his ear.

"Shido! Options!"

A window popped up on the airship *Fraxinus*'s main monitor, above the feed of Shido and the witchy Spirit. *Fraxinus*'s AI had determined three speech options suitable for the current moment.

1. "THERE'S ONLY ONE REASON. I CAME TO SEE YOU."

2. "I-I DON'T KNOW, EITHER. I DIDN'T RUN IN TIME, AND BEFORE I KNEW IT, I WAS HERE..."

3. "ANYWAY, WOULD YOU MIND LETTING ME FONDLE YOUR BOOBS?"

"Choices, people!" Kotori shouted from the captain's chair, and the crew, assembled on the lower deck, began to tap their consoles as one.

The aggregate results were soon up on the screen. One and two were neck and neck for top place; there were no votes for three.

"Well... I suppose that's reasonable," Kotori said, flicking the stick of her Chupa Chups back and forth.

"It has to be one!" Nakatsugawa snapped his fingers from below her. "Given that we don't know her temperament yet, it would be risky to act deliberately odd."

But Minowa's voice rose up in protest. "No, we should definitely go with two here. Nakatsugawa's a man, so perhaps he doesn't know this, but Shido surprisingly brings maternal instincts out in women! From the look of this Spirit, she's an older girl! We should make maximal use of this weapon!"

"Oh," Shiizaki said, softly, sounding like she was in agreement.

"Mm-hmm. I do get what you're saying. But it's a surprise that there are no votes for three. I was convinced Kannazuki would pick it as a bad joke." Kotori uncrossed and recrossed her legs as she looked back behind the captain's seat.

A tall man with a prominent nose was standing there with an impossibly serious face.

"Unthinkable," he said. "I am always in earnest."

"And how do you really feel then?" Kotori asked.

"The first gentle swellings of the chest are supreme," he declared. "I have no interest in slovenly breasts such as those."

"..."

"If one of the options had been 'please let me lick the backs of your knees,' I would have had a little trouble deciding."

"..."

Silently, Kotori beckoned him closer with a finger, made him bend down, and then spat the stick of her now finished Chupa Chups at his eye.

"Nooooooo!!" Kannazuki fell over backward, a hand pressed to his eye.

As she pulled a fresh Chupa Chups from her lollipop holder, Kotori flicked the switch to connect with Shido's earpiece. "Shido, two. Get some tears going and look up at her with real puppy dog eyes."

"Uh. Uhhh." Shido frowned at the instruction that came through his right ear. After all, he was in high school now. He very much didn't want to put on an act like he was a lost little kid.

"What's the matter?" The Spirit cocked her head at the change in expression on his face.

The last thing he needed was her getting suspicious. He needed to say something fast. With no other choice, he looked up at her with sad eyes just as Kotori had instructed and opened his mouth.

"Uh. Umm. I…have nooo idea. I didn't run away in time, and before I knew it, I was here…"

"…!"

The Spirit's eyes grew round. Her cheeks reddened ever so slightly, and the corners of her mouth slid upward. "Hmm. Is that so? And what's your name?"

"Uh. Shido Itsuka."

"Shido, hmm? Hee-hee-hee! Cute name."

"Umm. Uh. What's your name?" Shido asked awkwardly.

The Spirit smiled cutely. "I'm Natsumi. Although I guess you all call me Witch."

"Miss…Natsumi," he said, trying to play up the lost little boy angle.

"Hee hee! Just Natsumi is fine," she told him. "No need to stand on formality. I'm not too fond of all that stuff."

"Uhhh, okay, Natsumi," Shido said, and the Spirit—Natsumi—nodded with satisfaction.

"Oh," she said, as though she'd just remembered something, and clapped her hands together. "Right. Hee-hee-hee! I meant to ask the next time I saw a person."

She had no sooner whirled around than she was kicking out a heel with a *clack* and striking a pose. She turned her eyes back to Shido.

"Hey, Shido? There's something I want to ask. You mind?"

"Huh? Oh. No, go ahead," he replied, baffled.

"Shido." Natsumi ran a finger across her lips sexily and smiled at him. "Do you think I'm pretty?"

"Huh?" His eyes flew open at the unexpected question.

He didn't need to stop and think for an answer. She was obviously gorgeous. But why had she asked him this out of the blue? This was the real question. Maybe she had some ulterior motive or secret plan? He couldn't help but hesitate at this thought.

"*Shido, what are you doing?*" Kotori snapped. "*If you take too long, you run this risk of putting Natsumi in a bad mood.*"

She was right. Shido made his decision and turned back to the Spirit.

"Uh... Oh. I think you're super pretty."

"So I really am?!" Her face brightened as she pressed her hands to her cheeks and squirmed happily. "Hey, so, Shido? What specifically? What part of me's pretty?"

"Huh? Umm," he said. "Your almond eyes, maybe the perfect line of your nose."

"Uh-huh, uh-huh!" She urged him on with shining eyes.

"And you're tall. You have great style."

"Go on! What else?!"

"Your hair's so shiny and beautiful."

"Yes! You get it! You get me, Shido!" she cried, and hugged him tightly.

He felt her large breasts push up against him, and his face turned red. Natsumi appeared not to notice this, however, and began to hum happily, still hugging him.

But the pleased humming stopped abruptly, and for some reason, Natsumi got a sad look on her face.

"So *this* me is pretty then," she said, softly.

"Huh?" Shido frowned. What was *that* supposed to mean?

But before he could ask, Natsumi looked over her shoulder and said, "Oh dear."

"...?"

Shido lifted his face and followed her gaze.

In the sky reddened by the setting sun, he spotted several rough shadows in mechanical armor.

"The AST!" he cried.

Yes. The SDF's Anti-Spirit Team. With their objective being the elimination of the Spirits, they were in direct opposition to Ratatoskr.

Shido frowned. He couldn't see Origami in the AST formation deployed in a V in the sky, even though she was always in the
vanguard.

"Shido," Natsumi said. "You know the AST?"

"Ah!" His eyebrows shot up. He had maybe said too much.

But Natsumi didn't seem particularly concerned with that. Instead,
she patted Shido's head like she was praising a small child. "You're a
smart cookie. Look at you!"

"Uh. Right. Thanks," he replied with an awkward smile. This Spirit
was all over the place.

But he couldn't stand there idly forever now that the AST had
arrived.

"Shido! Get out of there!"

"…!"

Just as Kotori's shout rang in his ear, there was a flash in the sky, and
then a barrage of missiles was raining down on Shido and Natsumi.

"Wh-whoa!" he shouted, and reflexively shrank back.

But Natsumi chuckled nonchalantly, as she threw her right hand up
into the air and cried out, "C'mon, time to work, Haniel."

A broom-like object appeared from nowhere and settled into Natsumi's brandished hand. Although it looked like a broom, the bristled
end sparkled and glittered magically, as though adorned with precious metals and jewels.

An Angel. A Spirit's absolute weapon.

Natsumi spun the broom around and pointed the business end
toward the ground. The broom opened gently, and a dazzling light
spilled out as though it were reflecting the setting sun.

Poof!

He heard a silly sound, and the missiles barreling down on them
turned into cartoon-cute carrots.

"Huh?" Shido's eyes narrowed to stunned points in his face as he
watched the carrot missiles hit the ground with a ridiculous *BOMB!*
explosion like something out of a gag manga.

"Wh-what was that?" he asked, baffled.

"Just hang on a sec, okay, Shido?" Natsumi sat down on the broom and zoomed off into the sky, flying with an acrobatic flair.

"...! She's coming! Fire!"

The AST captain issued quick orders in response. The Wizards all squeezed the triggers on their weapons and rained bullets down on the broom-riding Spirit.

But Natsumi showed no signs of panicking. She raced around the sky and the bristled end of the broom produced a dazzling glow once more. The light radiated outward, swallowing up the AST members and the projectiles they fired.

"Wh-what's going on?!"

Bathed in the light, AST members and bullets alike were completely transformed. Now they were an assortment of rabbits and dogs and pandas and other adorable characters.

"Hee-hee-hee! You're all so much cuter this way!" Natsumi laughed as she turned in midair and returned to Shido.

The now hilarious-looking members of the AST were still up there, but totally confused by what had happened to them and no longer in control of their armor.

"All wrapped up," Natsumi said. "I was thinking of getting out of here and ditching these chumps while they're all a mess. You coming with, Shido?"

"Huh? Are you sure?" he asked.

"Of course. As long as you tell me more about how pretty I am, hmm?" Natsumi winked at him, adorably.

But then a carrot missile closed in on them from the sky above and hit the ground with the same funny noise as before.

"Whoa!" he yelped.

In terms of power, it didn't begin to compare with an actual missile. But because of the close range of the explosion, a cloud of dust puffed up around them. Dirt flew into Shido's eyes, and he was momentarily blinded.

"Aah! Ha...ha-choo!" Natsumi sneezed loudly, the dust no doubt tickling her nose.

Though his eyes were closed, Shido could tell that a bright light shone in front of him. Yes. Almost like Natsumi herself was glowing.

As soon as he thought it had faded, another bright light immediately filtered through his eyelids again.

"Mm." He rubbed his eyes and managed to get his lids open.

At the same time, an emergency alarm blared through his earpiece.

"Shido! Be careful! Natsumi's mood values are plummeting!"

"Huh?" Shido furrowed his brow at Kotori's words. The dust blanketing the area cleared away, and he could see Natsumi again.

For some reason, her face was bright red, and she was glaring hatefully at him.

"You saw that, huh?" she growled in a low voice, totally different from the way she had spoken thus far.

Shido raised his eyebrows, perplexed at the sudden change from the cheerful Natsumi of only moments ago. "S-saw what?"

"Don't play dumb! Just now, my... My...!" Natsumi clenched her jaw, straddled the broom in her hands, and bobbed up into the air. "Now that you've seen that, I can't let you walk away! Remember this. I will end your life!"

She pointed a finger at Shido, and then shot off into the distance.

"She's getting away! After her!" the AST captain called out.

Shido looked up and saw that the AST personnel were back to their normal selves. They spread their mechanical wings, got into formation, and chased after Natsumi.

"Wh-what on earth was that...?" Left alone, Shido could only stare up into the sky, baffled.

Chapter 2
Suspect

Monday, October 16.

Origami Tobiichi arrived at school and sighed as she sat down at her desk.

"..."

Hair that reached down to her shoulders. A slender physique. And a face like a doll's on which no expression could be read. But someone close to her might have noticed the faint hint of gloom that colored her features now.

The reason was simple.

The previous evening, a spacequake had been measured in the suburbs of Tengu, and an evacuation order issued. In other words, a Spirit appeared in this world. The AST had mobilized immediately and attacked the Spirit.

But Origami, who should have been considered an active AST member, could only obey the alarm, evacuate with everyone else to the shelter, and wait for the threat of the Spirit to pass.

Frustration consumed her. Knowing that she had the power to pull the trigger but wasn't allowed to was a major source of her restlessness. Origami, though normally composed, fought the rising swell of emotions spurred by this aggravation.

That said, this situation was the inevitable consequence of her actions.

First, she had taken the experimental weapon White Licorice without permission from where it sat peacefully in the hangar and used it to attack her allies. Then last month, she had equipped herself with an array of irregular equipment and bared her fangs at the DEM Wizards. As a result, while her superiors deliberated over her punishment, Origami was under suspension and prohibited from using any AST equipment.

Of course, her transgressions warranted disciplinary action, regardless of her reasons, and several criminal charges to boot. But the whole incident had been caused by irrational action on the part of DEM, and so more than a few voices were calling for Origami to be exonerated, and the discussions leading up to her punishment had dragged on. Despite all she'd done, Origami could be considered blessed.

However, this did not alleviate her anxiety.

There was one other reason for her agitation. A certain phenomenon had upset Origami's emotions.

"Shido," she said, in a voice too quiet for anyone else to hear, and looked to her right.

The seat there was empty. The desk of Origami's beloved, Shido Itsuka.

There was still time before morning homeroom started, though. It wasn't certain that Shido would be absent that day.

There was one more thing Origami wondered.

She stood up silently and walked over to the desk next to Shido's.

"Hmm?" The girl sitting there noticed Origami and glanced her way unhappily. "You? What do you want?" The girl—Tohka Yatogami—turned an almost-glare on Origami.

Origami had been wondering about this girl's presence in the classroom. Much to her chagrin, this girl lived near Shido, so they often came to school together.

"Shido's still not here?" Origami asked.

"Hmph!" Tohka scowled and then whipped her face away. "Hmph! I'm not telling you that Shido has a thing today, so he'll be a little late!"

"..."

Apparently, Shido had a thing that day, so he would be a little late.

Now that she knew this, there was no point in remaining there. Origami returned to her seat. She had no reason to speak with Tohka Yatogami unless pressed by necessity.

Perhaps sulking at Origami's attitude, Tohka stuck out her tongue at her. "Bleh!"

The rest of the class looked upon this exchange with well-worn exasperation.

Then the door to the classroom clattered open, and a boy came inside.

Neutral features, kind eyes. Yes. It was Origami's beloved, Shido Itsuka.

"Oh, Shido!" Tohka's expression changed completely as she exclaimed cheerfully and jumped to her feet.

Shido's eyebrows twitched in reaction, and he walked toward her.

"That was fast!" she said. "Did you finish your thing?"

"Yeah, thanks," he replied. "Anyway, you got a sec?"

"Mm-hmm. What?" Tohka cocked her head curiously.

Shido smiled gently, dropped his bag onto the floor, and with his now-free hands, grabbed Tohka's breasts.

"Mm? Hmm..." Tohka gaped for a second like she didn't understand what was happening. A beat later, her face turned red, and she launched a fist at his face. "Wh-wh-wh-wh-wh-wh-wh-wh-wh-what are you doing?!"

"Whoops!" But Shido dodged this blow splendidly and waggled his hands as though he were relishing the sensation of her chest. "Aah, those are some magnificent breasts! Squeezing the real deal just *feels* different."

"Wh-wh—!"

"Let me give them a squeeze in the raw next time?" He winked at her. "I'll be gentle."

"Wh-what are you talking about?! Are you out of your mind?!" Tohka said, stunned, cheeks tomato-red, as she clamped her arms over her chest.

Perhaps catching a bit of this commotion, the group of three girls chatting at desks nearby surrounded Shido with fierce glares.

Ai Yamabuki, Mai Hazakura, Mii Fujibakama. A well-known trio in grade eleven's Class Four and Tohka's good friends.

"Hey, Itsuka! What are you even doing?!"

"That's a straight-up crime, you know!"

"Want us to rip your fruit right off?!"

But Shido shrugged, indifferently, before taking the hand of Ai, who was closest, in a graceful movement and pressing her back against the wall. With his free hand, he gave her chin a nudge upward.

"I know you want me to play with you, too, but quit your squeaking," he said. "Or should I keep your mouth busy?"

"Whaaat?!" Ai's eyelids flew open, and she froze at this sudden counterattack.

Mai and Mii were also shocked by the unexpected development and gaped, forgetting to even try and stop Shido.

"N-no! I've got Kishiwada!" Ai tried resisting him, but Shido didn't stop. The distance between them shrank steadily, and Ai squeezed her eyes shut, her entire body tense.

Shido smiled, mischievously, and then brought his lips to her ear and blew gently.

"Ha-hanyaaa…" Ai's knees buckled, and she sank to the floor.

Mai and Mii finally came back to themselves with a gasp.

"A-Ai!"

"How dare you do that to Ai!"

They turned toward Shido with stern faces.

But Shido crouched down low, grabbed the hems of their skirts and flipped them up. A cry of "Ohhhhh!" rose up from the boys in the class, and Mai and Mii hurriedly pressed their skirts back down.

"Eeeaaaaaah!"

"Wh-what are you—how dare you?!"

"Ha-ha-ha! You're both wearing such cute underwear!" He smirked. "I'd love to get a more leisurely view of them in bed next time."

""Wha—?!""

Mai and Mii both turned beet red.

Shido threw up two fingers in a smug gesture. "Adieu," he said, slipping past the flustered girls with casual ease before leaving the classroom.

"Shido?" Origami frowned very faintly in the chaos he left in his wake.

◇

"Fwaaah." Yawning hugely, Shido walked down the hallway of Raizen High School.

The chime for the end of fourth period had apparently rung already; he could see girls walking with their bento lunches and boys making a dash for the school shop.

"Lunchtime already," Shido muttered to himself, scratching his cheek absently. "I'm seriously late."

He'd been forced to attend an emergency meeting on *Fraxinus* the day before. Normally, this sort of meeting ended in the middle of the night, but because they hadn't been able to glean anything on Natsumi's abilities or intentions, and because she'd made a statement about harming Shido somehow before she left, this particular planning session had gone on longer than usual.

Although he'd managed to sneak in a nap, he was far from fully rested. He rubbed his eyes gloomily with the back of his hand and yawned again as he climbed the staircase at school.

But when he opened the door to his classroom, Shido snapped wide awake.

""…!!""

His classmates all whirled around to look at him as soon as he stepped inside.

He jumped and glanced around in confusion, sweat springing up on his forehead. "Huh? Wh-what? What's going on, you guys…?"

The eyes of Ai-Mai-Mii flashed, and the girls charged toward him from where they were huddled together on the other side of the classroom.

"How dare you shamelessly march back in here, Shido Itsukaaaa!"

"You know what you did!"

"We will make you suffer and regret the fact that you were ever born!"

They surrounded Shido and began growling at him like wolves.

He unconsciously shrank back. This wasn't the first time the three girls had yelled at him, but he could see no reason for it that day. Not to mention, from the way they were talking, it sounded like Shido had been in this classroom earlier and done some evil deed to them.

"H-hang on a sec! Why on earth are you so angry?!" Shido said, spreading out his hands to placate the angry Ai-Mai-Mii. He had no idea what they didn't like about that, but their snarling grew even more vicious.

"Playing innocent isn't going to work here, buddy!"

"Yeah! There are plenty of witnesses!"

"You can't say you forgot that storm of cherry blossoms!"

Ai made a very unladylike gesture with her right hand, Mai swept an arm out to indicate everyone in the classroom, and Mii made a move like she would tear his jacket off but stopped before she did.

He still had no idea what they were talking about. Eyebrows tenting on his forehead, he looked around, pleading for help with his eyes.

"You mind, girls?"

He heard a familiar voice from behind Ai-Mai-Mii.

"Tohka!" His face brightened.

Lips pulled tight, Tohka stepped forward from between Ai and Mai to stand in front of Shido. He let out a sigh of relief.

"Thanks, Tohka. What's going on with those three anyway? I just got to school—"

However, Tohka flushed and hit Shido's stomach.

"Why would you do that randomly?" she said. "That, I mean... Of course I was surprised."

"Huh?" he said. "Wh-what are you talking about, Tohka? I didn't do anything."

"What?" She frowned and her expression grew hard. Tears in her eyes, she whapped Shido on the chest repeatedly.

"Ah!" he cried. "Wh-what, Tohka? That hurts."

"Shut up! I totally misjudged you, Shido! Maybe I could forgive you for that—*maybe*—but you won't even admit what you did!"

"No, seriously," he said. "What is the 'that' you're talking about?!"

"...! I-it's... You know. That. M-my...," Tohka stammered, her face growing even redder. She hung her head.

Ai-Mai-Mii threw their arms around her.

"It's okay! You'll be okay, Tohka!"

"Not only does he not admit his crimes, he forces the victim to relive their trauma!"

"There isn't a hell terrible enough for you!"

"No, seriously! What is going on?!" Shido shouted.

Someone grabbed his wrist.

"Huh?"

Origami Tobiichi had appeared next to him at some point. Her gaze was calm, but shining with a hard light that made him feel her determination.

"O-Origami? I didn't actually do something to you, too, did I?" Shido asked, ever-so-timidly.

Origami lowered her eyes and shook her head. "Nothing."

"O-oh okay." Shido relaxed his captured hand and let out a sigh.

But Origami tugged on his wrist, thrust his hand inside her—already unbuttoned—blouse and pressed it against her chest.

"Anggh?!" The sudden sensation made Shido produce a noise that had never come out of his throat before.

He tried to yank his hand back, but Origami had a solid grip on his wrist, and he couldn't move. Not only that, when he tried to fight back, a warm softness came through his sensitive palm and the tips of his fingers, turning his brain upside down.

"Wh-what are you doing?!" Tohka had recovered herself and ripped Origami's hand off Shido's wrist.

Shido hurriedly pulled back his now-free hand and took a deep breath to try and calm the furious drumming of his heartbeat. But with the warmth and feel and faintly alluring scent of Origami lingering on his hand, his face grew even redder.

"O-Origami? I thought I didn't do anything to you, though?" he asked, confused.

"Yes." Origami nodded. "So I'll ask you to do it now."

"H-huh?!"

"Do to me what you did to them. Press me up against the wall, lift my chin. Blow sweetly in my ear. Slowly lift my skirt."

"Wha—?!" His eyes flew open at the unpleasantly specific instructions, and the cheeks of Ai-Mai-Mii reddened in embarrassment.

Origami ignored them all and kept talking.

"And then give me a passionate kiss, rip my clothes off, steal my maiden purity, and stake your claim on my body so that I am marked by you for the rest of my life."

"Uh. Uhhh?!" Shido half-screamed.

"Origami Tobiichi! Shido didn't do any of that!" Tohka cried.

But Origami ignored them both and closed in on Shido. "Come on, Shido. Come on."

Hey. Uh. Umm…"

"Come on."

"S-sorryyyyyyyyyyyy!" Shido apologized for some reason as he fled.

Naturally, Origami reacted quickly to try and stop him from getting away, but Tohka blocked her way and began to fight with her about something.

Shido took advantage of this to run into the hallway, hoping to hide some place where they wouldn't be able to find him so easily.

Panting, he wiped away the sweat on his face.

"What were they even talking about? I only just got to school."

He frowned. The girls all spoke like he'd been there earlier, playing pranks on them.

He put a hand to his chin as he thought it over, when two girls with familiar faces stepped out in front of him. The sisters Kaguya and Yuzuru Yamai, from the class next door.

"Hey, Kaguya! Yuzuru—" He started to call out to them and then noticed something curious. For some reason, the girls weren't in their Raizen High School uniforms, but their school swimsuits. "Hmm?"

"Discovery. It's Shido."

Kaguya and Yuzuru raised their eyebrows at the same time as they noticed Shido. And then their gazes sharpened, and they both threw out their arms threateningly.

"At last, we locate you, Shido! So you remained within the school in lieu of fleeing! Hmph! I must at least praise your pluck!"

"Caution. We will not be caught off guard any longer. We will settle this debt right now."

"Wha—!" Shido tensed at this reaction from the twins and stepped backward. *What if...* "Y-you're not saying...I did something to you, too, right?"

Kaguya and Yuzuru frowned, dubiously.

"Do you intend to feign ignorance, Shido? Enough! Return to us the panties you pilfered!"

"Outrage. Who exactly was it who threw water on Yuzuru because he 'has a thing for see-through bras'?"

"E-eep?!" Shido was baffled, confronted with yet another crime he had no recollection of.

"I know not what you were thinking, but it's clear we must be ever vigilant with you."

"Assent. We panicked when our gym clothes were gone, but it was fortuitous that we left our pool bag."

"I-I would never—"

"You would claim innocence?! Impossible! That was most certainly you! I would not mistake your face!"

"Assent. That is correct. Kaguya would never mistake the face of the Shido she loves and adores."

"What are you talking about, Yuzuru?! If you're gonna say that, then you too—"

"Ignore. I have no idea what you're talking about."

The Yamai sisters then argued amongst themselves for a moment, but quickly shook their heads and turned back to Shido.

"At any rate! This will not pass! We will exact penance for the sin of spurning the Yamais from your flesh! Specifically, from Shido! Remove your underpants!"

"Concord. Additionally, Yuzuru will thoroughly spray your body with an atomizer."

The Yamai sisters slowly moved toward him.

"Y-you can't be serious?!" He couldn't accept retaliation for a crime he didn't commit. He whirled around, ready to run.

But before making his escape, he heard yet another familiar voice.

"Itsuka!"

A small woman with glasses. Although she looked to be young enough, she wasn't wearing a uniform, which meant that she wasn't a student. This was Shido's homeroom teacher, Tamae Okamine—aka Tama.

"T-Tama—I mean, Ms. Okamine." He hurriedly corrected the nickname he'd accidentally spoken.

Tama marched over to him and grabbed onto the hem of his shirt.

"Wh-what's wrong, Ms. Okamine?" he asked, a bad feeling in the pit of his stomach.

"Wh-what are you talking about after doing a thing like that!" Tama looked like she was about to burst into tears at any second. "N-no man will have me now… You will have to take responsibility for your actions and take me!"

"Wh-what?!" He had more or less expected something, but this was a leap too far. Shoulders shaking, he took a step backward.

And now a boy appeared from around the corner in the hallway. "Eep!" he cried, fearfully, as soon as he saw Shido.

It was Shido's best friend, Hiroto Tonomachi. Hair slicked back with gel and a traditionally masculine face. He was also blessed with a better physique than Shido. And yet he wrapped his arms around his shoulders in a girlish gesture for some reason, and his teeth began to chatter.

"T-Tonomachi?" Shido called, cautiously, and Tonomachi shook like a chihuahua.

"Itsuka... Sir. Umm. I... I do make a lot of jokes, so maybe there's been a misunderstanding... But I don't swing...*that* way..."

"What exactly happened to *you*?!" Shido cried, and perhaps surprised at his loud volume, Tonomachi pulled his head back just like a turtle.

"Ngh!" He didn't know what was going on, but the group gathered there clearly was not going to hear anything he had to say to try and clear his name. This was not a good place for him to be. He glanced around in search of an escape route.

"Huh?"

The moment he turned his gaze to the end of the hallway, Shido felt his blood run cold.

A boy was standing at the T-intersection where light poured in through the window. Slender physique, somewhat neutral features. Shido was overcome with a curious feeling that he had seen this face before. Or maybe not.

He quickly realized, however, that this was the face he saw every morning in the mirror.

Yes. It was impossible to believe, but Shido Itsuka stood there in front of him.

"..."

The other Shido glanced at Shido, and his lips curled up while he waved and walked down the hallway. It was practically a challenge.

"St-stop! Who are you?!" Shido shouted, and started to chase after the other Shido.

But he was no match for the instantaneous movement of the Yamai sisters. Kaguya caught his right arm, Yuzuru his left, and stopped him fast.

"Keh-keh! Did you think I would allow your escape? Abandon all hope, Shido! Repent your sins!"

"Confinement. We will not let you go. Now, we will devote our full attention to you."

"Hey! Hold on! I'm at the other end of the hallway!" He'd lose the other Shido like this. Making up his mind, he clenched his hands. "Aah! Fine! I'll be good!"

The Yamai sisters pinning his arms down nodded with satisfaction.

"Keh-keh! Oh? Excellent. You have dealt we Yamais an indignity. You will accept the deserved punishment."

"Assent. You should have done this from the start."

Kaguya and Yuzuru released his arms. They may have simply trusted Shido's words, but they were also confident they could easily catch him if he did try to flee. And on that point, they were correct. Although their powers were locked away at the moment, the Yamai sisters were originally Spirits that controlled the wind. Shido couldn't even begin to compare with their nimble feet. It would be extremely difficult to give them the slip.

Unless he successfully caught them off guard.

"Yeah, I give up. My underpants, right? I just have to take them off, right?!" Shido said as he began to fumble with his belt buckle.

"".…?!""

Kaguya, Yuzuru, and Tama jumped in surprise and half-reflexively covered their faces with their hands. Tonomachi, on the other hand, had gone pale and slid away along the wall.

This was his chance. While everyone had their hands over their faces, Shido raced after the other Shido.

He ran down the hallway and turned the corner where the other Shido had vanished. He caught sight of the imposter's back up ahead.

"There he is!" Shido clenched his teeth and ran faster toward that back.

Shido ran and ran around the school led on by the other Shido until eventually he came to the door to the roof.

"Haah! Haah! No…where! Left…to…run…" He put a hand on his

chest to try and get his breathing back under control. And then Shido put a hand on the knob and flung the door open.

The dim area was illuminated by a liberating blue sky.

But he didn't have time to admire the view. He stepped out onto the roof and looked around, searching every nook and cranny of the fenced-in area.

"'Sup. You're faster than I thought."

"…!"

Shido heard a voice from behind and stiffened. He looked back and saw a boy with exactly the same face as him sitting leisurely on the rooftop shed Shido had just come out of.

"You…really *are* me?!" Shido grimaced and glared at the other Shido.

Seeing the other boy up close, it was obvious that he hadn't been mistaken. He was a perfect copy of Shido, like he had stepped out of the mirror world.

"Heh-heh." The other Shido chuckled, leaped down from the shed, and landed in front of Shido.

Looking at him again, Shido was confused and also certain of one thing. The evil deeds Shido had no memory of carrying out testified to by Tohka, the three girls, Origami, the Yamai sisters, Tama, Tonomachi, and so many other people had most likely been the work of this other Shido before him now.

"Good guess. I had all kinds of fun while you weren't here."

Perhaps guessing at Shido's thoughts from the look on his face, the other Shido twisted his lips up. His voice and mannerisms were a perfect match. Every word he spoke caused an unfathomable unease to grow in the pit of Shido's stomach.

"You… What *are* you? How can you have my face? And what do you want?!" Shido said, glaring and on guard, and the other Shido chuckled like it was all so hilarious he could hardly stand it. "I-is something funny?!"

"Heh-heh! Well, of course, it's funny. I mean, you still haven't caught on. Silly Shido."

"Wha..." Shido gasped and his eyes flew open.

That last comment from the other Shido was in a woman's voice, totally different from Shido's. And it was a voice he'd heard somewhere before. Recently.

"That voice... No way... Natsumi?"

Yes. There was no doubt that this was the voice of the Spirit Natsumi Shido had encountered the day before.

The other Shido grinned, bewitchingly, and gave him the OK sign with thumb and forefinger. "Ding-ding-ding! Correct. Well done. Look at you!"

"Wh-why are you..." As he started to ask, the scene he witnessed the previous day popped up clearly in his mind.

Haniel, the Angel Natsumi manifested. The missiles and AST members showered in its light were all forced into new forms. The ability to change objects into other things. If she could apply that power to her own body, then her current form made sense.

But now that he'd figured this out, there was something else he didn't get.

"What exactly are you after?" he demanded, a stern look on his face. "Turning into a copy of me, playing tricks on everyone!"

The other Shido—Natsumi—abruptly dropped the merry grin and returned his glare. "You really don't know? Really?"

"Wh-what..." Shot through by Natsumi's sharp gaze, Shido felt like his heart was being squeezed.

At the same time, the words she had spoken when they parted the day before came back to life in his ears.

Now that you've seen that, I can't let you walk away! Remember this. I will end your life!

"Oh!" Shido's eyebrows shot up, and he swallowed hard. "Y-you're not actually going to end my life?"

"Twenty points," Natsumi replied, rolling her eyes.

"Huh?"

"I told you, didn't I? No one gets to just walk away after learning my secret. Do you think I'll let it go with this level of harassment? Don't be ridiculous. I'm not gonna stop until I make an absolute, awful, appalling mess out of your life!"

"H-hang on a minute. I don't actually know your—" Shido started, exasperated, but Natsumi kicked at the roof loudly to cut him off.

"See? There we go. No one who knows my secret is allowed to live in this world."

"...?!"

Overwhelmed by the rage on Natsumi's face and her abnormal force, Shido unconsciously took a step back.

But paying this no mind, Natsumi pointed a finger at him, an exquisite smile spreading across her lips. "But don't worry. After all, see? There are two Shidos here. And it's weird for there to be two of the same person, riiight? That just means I have to make sure there's only one."

"Only one... You don't mean...?!"

Fear transformed Shido's face, and Natsumi nodded leisurely, grin still plastered on her face.

"Starting today, I'll be Shido. Starting today, I'll *perform* Shido. You don't need to worry about anything. I'm an excellent observer, and I've done my research. Looked into you and your relationships. I won't play any more games like the ones before. I'm sure no one will even notice you're gone. The world will carry on unchanged even when you're gone."

Natsumi continued, gesturing and moving like she was performing on stage.

"Hee hee! Relax. I'm not going to kill you or anything. I'm just going to have you go somewhere you can't get in my way."

"Y-you can't be serious!" Shido cried out, wildly. "That's—"

Slam!

The door to the roof flew opened, and two girls poked their faces out.

Tohka and Origami.

"You! You go somewhere else! *I'm* going to find Shido!"

"I could say the same to you. I can't leave this to someone like you. Hurry back to the classroom."

Apparently, they were looking for him. The two girls glared at each other as they pushed and shoved their way onto the roof.

But then they realized someone else had beaten them to it. They froze at the same time, and their eyes grew round like they couldn't believe what they were seeing.

"T-two...Shidos?"

"Meaning?"

Tohka and Origami spoke in tandem, brows knit suspiciously, and looked back and forth between Shido and Natsumi. Well, that was only natural. After all, there were two people with the same face standing in front of them.

But in a certain sense, this was also his chance. Now that the girls had witnessed this decisive proof, they would understand that it hadn't been the real Shido playing all those tricks.

"Tohka! Origami! Listen to me! This is—"

"He's the fake!" Natsumi cried out loudly, cutting Shido off. Naturally not in her own voice, but in a perfect copy of Shido's. "He's the one who impersonated me and played all those pranks on everyone!"

"Wha—! Don't be fooled! I'm the real Shido!"

"What are you talking about? *I'm* the real Shido!"

Tohka and Origami frowned slightly. They were apparently confused about which was the real Shido.

But Shido could only continue his desperate appeal. He turned toward them and kept going.

"Tohka, Origami, you have to believe me! *I'm* the real Shido Itsuka!"

"Don't let him trick you! Please! You have to trust me!" Natsumi also cried out, desperately. Even Shido thought she looked like the real him.

"Mm. So this means that one of them is a fake? Then..."

"An impossible situation. But..."

Tohka and Origami compared Shido and Natsumi for a moment, and then each of them raised an index finger.

"You're the fake."

"You. Fake."

At the exact same moment, they snapped those index fingers out. Toward the fake Shido. Natsumi.

"Wha...?!" Natsumi was stunned. She hadn't imagined they would be able to discern the genuine article without the slightest uncertainty like this. But she couldn't let it go. "Wh-what are you talking about? I'm..."

Tohka and Origami showed no signs of rethinking their decision. They shook their heads and came over to Shido.

Natsumi finally gave up and glared venomously at them. "How'd you tell? My transformation was perfect. Guessing at random would've only been fifty-fifty. How can you be so confident and point at me?"

Tohka and Origami met each other's eyes before speaking in turn.

"I mean...I just am," Tohka said, vaguely. "You *do* look like Shido, but when you're standing next to the real thing, I feel like you smell different or something. That's all."

"If you had been here alone, then maybe I would have been deceived. I did actually think you were Shido before. But if we're talking about two Shidos and which one is the real one, that's a different story. You blink zero point zero five seconds faster than the real Shido, and your center of gravity is zero point two degrees to the left of Shido's. I could never mistake you for him," Origami explained at length.

"Wh-what..." Natsumi/Shido looked at them like she couldn't believe what she was seeing. "What is *with* these girls?! Something's wrong with them!"

"Oh, well, that's...yeah," Shido mumbled. They had easily picked out the fake. Naturally, he was grateful to them, but he also felt like he could understand Natsumi's surprise.

Natsumi gritted her teeth in annoyance and threw her hands up. The broom-shaped Angel appeared out of thin air, and she had no sooner grabbed onto it than the tip was fanning open to emit a glow like a reflection of the sun.

In the next instant, Natsumi shone faintly and turned into the beautiful, tall girl Shido had seen the day before.

"Wha…?!"

"…!"

Tohka and Origami gaped and pulled back slightly as they crouched down, seemingly to protect Shido.

But Natsumi paid them no mind. She clenched her teeth together with vexation and clawed at her head.

"Impossible… Impossible… Impossibleeeeee!"

"Wha…"

"First, you learn my secret, and now you see through my perfect transformation? No… It can't be! I won't… There's no way!" Natsumi shouted, hatefully, and snapped a finger out at Shido and the girls. "This isn't over! I will absolutely get you back…I'll give you the shock of your life!"

She jumped onto the broom, leaped up from the roof, and flew off into the sky.

"Aaah! Hey!" Shido cried out in a panic and ran toward her, but he was too late.

Without so much as a glance back at him, Natsumi's silhouette grew smaller in the distance.

"Ngh…"

He was supposed to be getting his likability with her up and sealing her Spirit powers, but the whole thing had ended in him making zero progress.

That said, however, it had been an entirely unexpected encounter. She had shown up without warning and tried to take his place. It was a bit much. He would have to report to Kotori.

But it seemed there was something else he had to do first.

"Shido."

"Shido."

Tohka and Origami had vigilantly watched the sky until Natsumi disappeared completely, and now they both looked back at him.

"Wh-what? Why are you looking at me?" Shido replied, in a tense voice, having more or less guessed at what they would say next.

"Who was that?!"

"Who's that woman? What's your relationship?"

They said almost exactly the words he was expecting.

His face tightened and he racked his brain trying to figure out how he could explain this situation without telling them who Natsumi was.

DEM Industries, UK head office.

Several men were assembled in a conference room on the twentieth floor. All of them were on DEM's board of directors. They sat around an enormous elliptical table with complex expressions on their faces as they sifted through the papers in front of them.

However, that was to be expected.

They had already received reports from a number of sources. The documents at hand merely noted the particulars of the incident.

After DEM's managing director, Isaac Westcott, had improperly wielded his authority in Japan, the DEM Japan branch office and its associated facilities had been half-destroyed. Not to mention the fact that a number of their precious Wizards had been injured or killed, and the cherry on top was that their secret Realizer technology had been on full display for everyone in the area to see. Anyone who could go through these reports and not so much as arch an eyebrow should probably immediately quit the company and take up a new career gambling.

However, not everyone looked upset. One man sat leisurely in the chair at the farthest end of the room.

He was a young man in his mid-thirties, wearing a jet-black suit. Disturbingly dark eyes peered out through the gaps of the dark gray hair which hung down across his forehead, looking out at the conference room. Sir Isaac Ray Pelham Westcott. The very DEM Managing Director who was the subject of discussion.

"What on *earth* were you thinking, Westcott?!" one board member cried out wildly, hand shaking as he slammed the documents in it against the table. He was a middle-aged man with glasses. He was one of the younger directors, but even so, he appeared to be older than Westcott.

No one in the room reproached him for his aggression toward the MD. Although their feelings varied in degree, everyone was thinking the same thing.

But Westcott himself, looking out at them from his seat at the end of the table, didn't seem the least bit flustered. He merely shrugged, slightly. "I don't understand the intent of the question, Murdock."

"I ask that you not play dumb with us!" Murdock yanked up the papers he'd thrown onto the table to brandish them in front of his face. "Improper interference with the SDF, personal use of Wizards and equipment, instructions for an attack mission that would endanger the general populace, turning a corner of the business district into a battlefield?! At minimum, the cost of the damage is one billion pounds! And now the Japanese government has something significant on us! How exactly do you intend to rectify this situation?!"

"Not a problem," Westcott said. "We got results in line with the scale of damage."

"Results? And what would those be?" Murdock demanded.

The corners of Westcott's mouth slid up. "Rejoice. We succeeded in inverting Princess."

"…!"

Murdock and the other board members stared in wide-eyed surprise at Westcott's evident pride.

"Are you serious?! Do you not understand the situation here?!" Murdock shouted, his face colored with anger. "One wrong step, and this could very well develop into a threat to the continued existence of DEM Industries! What is this about a Spirit? How exactly will a Spirit save our company in a crisis?! We are *through* going along with your little games and smug self-satisfaction!"

"Oh?" Westcott wore a mechanical smile on his face, but now one of his eyebrows twitched ever so slightly.

But Murdock apparently didn't notice. He turned to look at the board members gathered in the conference room.

"I'd like to ask all of you one simple question! Can we actually allow him to continue to do whatever he pleases? If this keeps up, DEM Industries will be ruined in the not-so-distant future! We should be taking measures to ensure that doesn't happen!"

"Measures?" the man sitting across from Murdock asked.

Murdock threw out his arms theatrically and proclaimed, "I. Am. *Demanding* the dismissal of Managing Director Westcott, right here and now!"

"—!"

The board members jumped in their seats. Some looked astounded at the demand for dismissal, but more than half of them looked as though they had known about it in advance.

Murdock nodded, assured, as he looked out at their faces, and turned to the elderly man sitting next to Westcott. "Chairman Russell. Your decision."

At British companies, the managing director was not permitted to also act as the chair of the board of directors. In other words, on paper at least, there needed to be a representative of the board other than Westcott. This was the chair, Russell.

"Is this acceptable, sir?" With a troubled look on his face, Russell glanced over at Westcott.

But Westcott looked entirely unconcerned. "Of course. That is the formal authority given to the board of directors."

"..."

Russell lowered his eyes and sighed as though guessing at something before raising his voice. "Well then. We shall take it to vote. All those in favor of dismissing MD Westcott, raise your hands."

Murdock threw his hand into the air, and other board members followed suit, raising their hands one after another. The majority were younger members.

This was clearly an unusual situation.

Westcott's actions had indeed sent extremely large waves rippling through the company, and more than a few of the directors were increasingly dissatisfied with his arrogant behavior. But it was hard to imagine that more than half of them would be in agreement with Murdock in a supposedly sudden vote.

Westcott looked at Murdock, who sniffed triumphantly as a sneer spread across his lips. Most likely, he had talked to people in secret before Westcott returned to England.

Russell sent his gaze around the conference room to count the hands in the air and said, quietly, "Given that we have zero hands in favor, the request to dismiss MD Westcott is rejected."

"What?" Murdock furrowed his brow. "Set aside the jokes, Russell. You must think of your pride as the chair. Or is it that your eyesight has gotten so poor that you can't see the number of hands up?"

"No," Russell told him. "I am merely telling you the results as I see them."

"What?" Murdock said, doubting his ears, and looked up. And gasped.

Following his gaze, the other directors with their hands up also screwed up their faces in anguish.

It was unavoidable.

Their raised arms were gone from the elbow.

"Ungh. Ah! Ah! Aaaaaaaaaaaaaaaaah?!" Murdock screamed and crumpled to the floor, as if only feeling pain now that he noticed his sudden lack of a hand. Fresh blood began to gush from the smooth cross section below his elbow.

The conference room was instantly transformed into the very portrait of an agonizing hell.

"Games? Smug superiority?" A calm voice came from behind Westcott. "Quite the statement from someone who only came aboard after Ike elevated the DEM name, hmm?"

A girl with pale blond hair stepped forward, seeming quite out of place at this meeting. In one of her hands, she held a laser edge about the size of a paring knife.

Given that she was able to maintain a blade on the laser edge without a wiring suit, something that was generally considered impossible, and that on top of that, she had been able to extend the blade into a long, thin thread to cut off the hands of the board members all at once, the extent of her abilities was quite obvious.

Ellen M. Mathers. Head of the second enforcement division, which wielded the real power behind the scenes at DEM, and the most powerful Wizard in the world.

"Now, don't say that, Ellen," Westcott chided her. "He was simply and quite naturally taking advantage of the situation in which he'd been placed, and exercising the authority given to him."

"But..." Ellen persisted, and Westcott stopped her as he stood up slowly.

"Medical Realizers are on standby in the medical office. If you reattach the limbs right away, you'll no doubt be back to your old selves in a few days. Go. You're all excellent human resources, shouldering the future of DEM. Don't you think it would be rather absurd to lose an arm over a thing like this?"

"...! You!" Dropping all pretense of politeness, Murdock glared at Westcott.

But Westcott ignored him. "Have no fear. Once my *little games* and *smug self-satisfaction* reach their natural conclusion, I'll hand this company over to all of you. And you won't even have to wait nearly as long as *we* have to get this far." He laughed quietly.

"Aah," Shido griped with a sigh and threw his legs up on the arm of the sofa.

Saturday, October 21. It had already been five days since Natsumi showed up at school pretending to be him, and he hadn't seen her once since then. There had been no spacequakes, and *Fraxinus*'s measurement devices hadn't picked up any trace of her.

"It's actually worse that she's doing nothing." He put a hand to his forehead and sighed again as he lay on the sofa.

While he was staring up at the ceiling, deep in through, he felt something heavy land on his stomach abruptly.

"Hngh! Wh-what the…?" Scowling at the sudden load, he dropped his gaze down toward his abdomen. And found his little sister Kotori sitting there with a smile.

"Hey, Kotori."

She flicked the stick of the Chupa Chups in her mouth around as she smiled daringly and turned her eyes toward Shido. "Oh dear! You were so lacking in vitality that I thought this was an unusual human leather sofa."

"We don't have any Ed Gein-type furniture made of people in our house, okay?" Shido said, rolling his eyes, and Kotori pushed her weight into his stomach before standing up. "Hyangh!"

"Oh my, did I maybe hit the jackpot there?" Kotori smiled.

"Listen, you…" Shido slowly sat up, rubbing his stomach.

"Hmph. You're being targeted by a Spirit, and here you are loafing about. We don't know what she's planning. Wouldn't kill you to be a little more on guard."

"Ngh…" He couldn't say anything to that. He bit his lip and fell silent.

"We don't know what that Spirit—Natsumi—is thinking, but it's hard to imagine she'll do nothing and simply fade away. She'll make contact with you somehow. And given that we have no way of contacting her, we have to make sure to get your likability up with her when she decides to come around. You do actually understand this, don't you?"

"Y-yes," Shido replied.

"I wonder." Kotori shrugged in exasperation.

But she was exactly right. The objective of Shido, Kotori, and the rest of Ratatoskr was not to defeat the Spirits, but to peacefully seal their powers away and allow them to lead normal lives. So something like the current situation in which a Spirit was hostile to Shido for some reason or another was normally to be avoided at all costs.

And in the case of Natsumi, they had no idea why she had decided he was her mortal enemy. They needed to turn the tables when she made contact and figure out the reason for this. They had a world of problems.

Perhaps noting the expression on Shido's face, Kotori sniffed and brandished the envelope she held in her hand. "You've finally got the right look of tension. Here. This was in the post this morning."

"Huh?" Shido took the envelope, cocking his head curiously. Once he had it in hand, he could tell that it had a surprising heft to it.

The front of the white envelope read only "Mr. Shido Itsuka." There was no address or postal code, and no stamp. Mostly likely, the sender had dropped it directly into the Itsuka postbox.

"Is this…a letter?" he said.

"Yes. A love letter," Kotori replied. "From Natsumi."

"Wha—?!" His eyes flew open in surprise, and he hurried to look at the back of the envelope.

It was neatly sealed with wax, and below that, there was indeed the name "Natsumi."

Shido swallowed to wet his dry throat, put the letter on the table, and sat up straight. "I-is it okay to open?"

"Yes. It seemed within the realm of possibility that it might explode or something the second you open it, so I had *Fraxinus* examine it from the outside," Kotori told him. "There's nothing dangerous inside. Of course, given that we're up against a Spirit here, there's no absolute guarantee of that."

"…"

Shido stiffened, and he broke out in a sweat.

Still, he couldn't just leave the envelope unopened. Digging deep, he gave himself a silent pep talk, and then removed the seal and pulled the contents of the envelope out.

"This is…"

"Looks like pictures, huh?" Kotori said, suspiciously, peering at the objects in Shido's hand.

Yes. The envelope contained a number of photographs.

It felt sort of weird to get photos from a Spirit, but if Natsumi had been coming and going quietly from this world like she had the other day, it made sense that she would take photos and know all kinds of things about life on this side.

And either way, the real issue was the subject of the pictures.

"Is that me?" Kotori picked one up with a frown.

It did indeed show Kotori in her junior high uniform, hair tied up in white ribbons. But she wasn't looking at the camera, and it had been taken from a distance. Almost like... Judging from Kotori's reaction, there was no doubt that this had been taken without her knowledge.

And it wasn't just Kotori. There were a total of twelve photos in the envelope, and all of them were full-body shots of people close to Shido—Tohka, Origami, Kotori, Yoshino, Kaguya, Yuzuru, Miku, Ai, Mai, Mii, Tama, and Tonomachi. All taken without the subject knowing they were being photographed. (Except for Origami, who was turned toward the camera as though she had noticed it.)

"Wh-what up with these pictures?" Shido scowled, creeped out. What exactly was Natsumi trying to say by sending him something like this?

"It's just the photos?" Kotori asked. "Nothing else?"

"R-right." Shido dug around in the envelope and found one more thing inside, a card. He pulled it out and set it on the table.

*"I'm in here. Can you guess who I am? Before anyone disappears.
Natsumi"*

Chapter 3
Delete

The next day, October 22, 10:59 AM.

Shido stood in front of the Itsuka house, looking at the time displayed on his cell phone.

It was a crisp fall day, a bit chilly for short sleeves. From time to time, a brisk breeze rustled the red leaves of the trees and caressed his cheeks as it passed up into the sky.

"Shido!"

Just as the time changed to 11:00, he heard a bright voice from the entrance to the apartment building rising up next to the Itsuka house.

When he looked in that direction, Tohka was waving innocently and running over to him, wearing her fall uniform. He raised his hand in response.

"Sorry," she said. "Were you waiting?"

"No, you're right on time," he told her. "I'm the one who should be sorry, asking you out of the blue like this."

"Don't worry about it! Anyway, where are we going shopping today?!" Tohka asked, eyes shining.

The night before, Shido had told her he wanted her to come shopping with him.

"Oh. Right." He nodded. "How about we head for the station to start?"

"Mm!" Tohka said, enthusiastically. She looked like she was so excited about going out with Shido that she could hardly stand it.

Happiness, embarrassment, fondness, and all kinds of other emotions swirled inside of Shido, and he smiled awkwardly.

"*...Shin, don't forget today's objective, okay?*"

At the sound of Reine's voice suddenly in his right ear, Shido jumped a little.

"R-right," he replied, quietly, and glanced at Tohka walking next to him. The usual Tohka, her usual face. Nothing out of the ordinary.

Except maybe.

"..."

Shido gulped.

The image of the other Shido at school a few days ago flitted through the back of his mind.

Yes. This Tohka could be a fake—an impersonation by Natsumi.

Staring at her face silently, Shido recalled the conversation he'd had with Kotori the day before.

"'I'm in here. Can you guess who I am,'" Kotori said, looking troubled, as she stared at the card that had been in the envelope with the pictures.

"Wh-what does that mean?" he asked.

"...Well..." Kotori had called Reine down from *Fraxinus* to discuss the situation. She lined up the twelve photos on the table as she said, "...If we take it at face value, it means that Natsumi has turned herself into one of these twelve people."

"...!"

Shido gasped. Although he had more or less guessed that.

The ability he'd seen Natsumi use, the Angel's power to reproduce Shido's exact appearance—she could easily use that to turn into someone else, too.

"And she's saying I have to try and guess who she's turned into," he said, slowly.

"That is what it looks like, hmm?" Kotori said, crossing her arms. "That last bit about before someone disappears concerns me a bit, though."

Shido swallowed hard. "So basically…there's a time limit?"

"That might well be it," Kotori agreed. "To be honest, we don't have enough information to go on."

"…At any rate, we need to get moving right away," Reine said, troubled, as she looked at the photos and put a hand to her mouth.

"Get moving? I mean, what exactly do we do?" Shido asked.

"Right." Kotori flicked up the stick of the Chupa Chups in her mouth. "First, Ratatoskr will check for a Spirit signal on everyone in the photos. We're up against a Spirit who wields consummate power. It'd really speed things up if there was even a hint of Spirit power radiating from one of them."

"Makes sense." Shido nodded.

Reine opened her mouth, as if to pick up where Kotori left off. "But we should assume that it'll be extremely unlikely to detect a Spirit signal. So in tandem with that, we'll be putting you to work as well, Shin."

"Okay. What do you want me to do?" Shido said as he clenched his hands into fists. Although he still didn't know how, this had all started because Shido upset Natsumi somehow when they first met. And now she'd dragged his friends into it. He couldn't just sit back and watch.

However.

"…Let's see," Reine said. "Given the situation, you could decide on an order for the dates."

"…Huh?" Shido responded, idiotically. "Date…? Wh-what do you mean?"

"Just what she said," Kotori responded, quite indifferently. "You'll be going on dates with each of the twelve people in these photos, starting tomorrow. And you'll check if something feels off with them."

"…! I-I get it!" he said.

Natsumi might have had the ability to transform into anyone and reproduce external elements like appearance and voice, but in an actual conversation, he might be able to pick up on cues that the person was different from their usual self.

That didn't mean he was home free, however.

"But look at all these pictures," Shido said, sweat soaking his brow. "Dates with everyone, huh?"

"...Mm-hmm," Reine replied. "Of course, you won't be able to get to all of them in a single day. Even if you hurry, three or four people a day is probably the limit."

"No, that's not it." He shook his head. "I mean, Tohka and them are one thing. But this means I have to ask Yamabuki, Hazakura, Fujibakama, Tama, and even...Tonomachi out on dates, right?"

Kotori shrugged in exasperation. "Come on, now's really not the time for that, is it? In fact, that way of thinking might be playing right into Natsumi's hands."

"Ungh. I-I guess," Shido stammered.

Reine nodded, slightly. "...Of course, we'll give you the maximum support possible. Out of Natsumi's sight, though."

"Okay," he said. "And you have to back me up again this time, too, Kotori."

But Kotori only frowned.

Reine spoke up. "...Oh, sorry, but Kotori can't be part of the back-up crew this time."

"Huh?" He raised an eyebrow. "She can't?"

"Well, of course I can't. I mean, I'm one of the suspects," Kotori said, sniffing imperiously.

Shido's eyes flew open. "Oh!"

"...That's how it is. I'll be taking the lead on this one. Sorry, Kotori. But until we determine who Natsumi is, we can't let you onto *Fraxinus*."

"Mm-hmm. A necessary measure. No way around it." Kotori nodded, surprisingly fine with Reine's decision. She had no doubt anticipated this the moment she saw her own photo in the envelope from Natsumi.

And it made sense to keep her off the ship. Although he hadn't noticed anything off about Kotori during their conversation, given that there was a non-zero chance that she was Natsumi, she couldn't be allowed into the heart of Ratatoskr. He shivered in fear at the thought of a hostile Spirit suddenly appearing on the bridge. Given that Reine was not among the suspects, she was the logical choice to provide support on this mission.

"But I wonder why you aren't in here, Reine," he said. "I mean, Tama and Yamabuki and the others are."

"…Mm. This is absolutely nothing more than a guess," she said. "But it's probably because I wasn't around when Natsumi was choosing her potential targets. I've been holed up on *Fraxinus* doing the analysis on Natsumi."

"Oh." He nodded. "Makes sense."

"…Well, of course, it could also just be that I didn't measure up in Natsumi's eyes, though," Reine said, with a self-deprecating shrug.

Hard-pressed with how to respond to this joke, Shido simply offered a weak smile.

Kotori cleared her throat as if to get the conversation back on track. "Anyway. A win for us is to make Natsumi weak in the knees and seal her Spirit powers. Make sure you pay very careful attention to every little detail."

She scowled in annoyance and clenched her jaw.

"If Natsumi's mood destabilizes any more than this, then not only will we not be able to seal her, but we might risk a hostage situation."

"…?!" Shido felt his heart constrict. "H-hang on a minute. What hostage?"

"…Think about it," Reine told him. "Natsumi's telling you to find her in among these people. If there are two people with the same face, then that dramatically narrows it down."

"…! Then…" Fear colored Shido's face.

Reine was exactly right. After all, when Natsumi had turned into Shido, it was only when she was standing next to the real Shido that Tohka and Origami could pick out the genuine article. She wouldn't make the same mistake twice.

In which case, what would she do? The answer was extremely simple.

"She'll have locked up the person she's impersonating somewhere," Shido said, reluctantly.

"I guess that's what'll happen," Kotori agreed, scowling. "We've got no wiggle room here. We'll split all twelve up over three days and do whatever it takes to find Natsumi."

"Yeah. I'm definitely going to find her." Shido clenched his fists and nodded, firmly.

And so there he was, on a date.

Shido glanced over at Tohka.

"Hmm? Something wrong, Shido?"

"Oh, no, nothing…"

Tohka met his eyes abruptly, and he looked away awkwardly. Scratching his cheek, he quickened his pace a tiny bit.

It wasn't just her face, body, or voice—the way she tilted her head, her gestures that were reminiscent of a small animal, all of it was perfectly and completely the Tohka in Shido's memory. At the very least, she didn't seem like a fake.

But wasn't that very perfection actually suspect? His head spun in confusion.

Perhaps picking up on this, Reine spoke through his earpiece, "… *Relax. If Natsumi did turn into Tohka, you're not going to catch her by acting normally. It might be good for you to try and shake her up a bit.*"

"What do you mean?" Shido replied, in a quiet voice, and sank into thought before turning his gaze toward Tohka once again. "H-hey, Tohka? How long's it been since the two of us went out together like this?"

"Hmm? Where'd that come from?" Tohka turned curious eyes on him.

"Oh, just popped into my head." Shido waved his hand, absently. "I was thinking we haven't really been alone together lately."

"We haven't? I feel like we went to get groceries a couple days ago, though."

"Oh. Did we?" Shido nodded to himself. They had gone to do the shopping the day he met Natsumi. It seemed that she clearly remembered that.

"But you know, that's that," she added, quickly with a guileless smile, perhaps misinterpreting his silence. "I think it's good to go out as many times as we can. Mm-hmm, I'm super happy today. It's going to be fun."

Shido's own face grew hot at how adorable she looked. But now was not the time for that.

He forced a bold smile and swallowed hard before opening his mouth. "Pretty amazing work. The spitting image of Tohka. Hmm, *Natsumi*?"

"…!"

Tohka jumped and stopped in her tracks.

Shrinking slightly at her reaction, Shido also came to a stop.

He didn't have any actual proof. It was just a stab in the dark. He actually thought that even if this Tohka was a fake created by Natsumi, she might not react to his leading question at all.

But the way Tohka was reacting… She couldn't actually be…

Shido stiffened, nervously, as Tohka slowly turned toward him, eyes filled with a level of hostility he couldn't imagine in the real Tohka.

"No way. You're really…?"

However.

"Shido. Who is this 'Natsumi'?" she demanded. "Did you just call me by another girl's name?"

"Huh?" Shido felt his clenched fist loosen.

Tohka wasn't upset that her true identity had been found out; she was simply unhappy.

"*…Shin. You are supposedly in the middle of a date. I think it's only natural that she would be upset at being called by another girl's name.*"

"Oh. I-I guess you're right," he murmured, nervously, and he spread out his hands to placate the deeply suspicious Tohka. "S-sorry. Come on, you know. Haven't you ever heard anyone say 'natsuumi'? It's this greeting from the Dominican Republic that's pretty popular lately."

"It is?" she asked, her face softening.

Of course, he was completely making this up. Shido internally apologized to the Dominican people as he nodded.

"Hmm," she said, thoughtfully. "What's it mean?"

"Uh. Umm. Something like, I love you," he replied, randomly.

"Mm!" Tohka's cheeks reddened slightly. "Mm... Oh, really? Hee hee!"

It seemed Shido had dodged that bullet. He let out a sigh of relief.

But then her shoulders stiffened again. "So what was that whole 'spitting image of Tohka' part?"

"Huh? Oh. Umm, that was..." Shido stammered, unable to think up a decent lie. He could see her eyes start to narrow, suspiciously, again.

"*...This is bad*," Reine interjected. "*It's all over if Tohka gets upset. Can't you do something to put her in a better mood again?*"

"Do something? It's not that easy." Shido's eyebrows drew together as he looked around. "Oh! H-hey, Tohka? You haven't had lunch yet, right? It's a bit early, but how about we go grab a bite?"

He pointed to a restaurant on the other side of the road. Below the sign with the name was a poster that read *Lunch buffet open now!*

"Hmm? Lunch? Well...sure, I guess," Tohka said, still pouting. Normally, her eyes would shine with excitement at the thought of lunch, but well, he supposed he'd have to take this.

With Tohka trailing behind him, a troubled look on her face, Shido entered the restaurant.

Given that it was lunchtime, it was fairly busy, but fortunately, they were able to get a table right away. He tossed his bag under his chair and looked at Tohka across from him, as he wiped his hands. "So, Tohka. This place has a buffet. You go ahead and get a plate first."

"Mm." Her face brightened for a second, but then she shook her head as if she'd remembered something. "I'll go after you, Shido."

"Huh?" He frowned. "Why?"

"Because. So hurry up. Go." Tohka stubbornly refused to yield.

"O-okay." Shido stood up. "What's up with her anyway?"

"*...I don't know. But if you just do what she wants here, you should be in the clear*," Reine said.

"I guess," Shido replied, before walking over to the area with all the different meals on display. He picked up a plate, filled it with a bunch of different things, and returned to their table.

However, maybe because of his nerves and the pressure to find Natsumi, he didn't exactly have much of an appetite. The plate he brought back had little more than a bit of salad and some grilled chicken on it.

"Okay, you go and get yours, Tohka," he said.

"…Mm." Tohka gave his plate a hard look before standing up.

He cocked his head to the side as he watched her go. He had thought she was still thinking about his slip-up from before. But this felt different somehow. What exactly could put that cloudy look on her face at mealtime?

While he was thinking about this, Tohka returned, unexpectedly quickly. She set the plate in her hand on the table and sat down.

"Okay, how about we start eating then?" she said.

"Yeah, you bet." Shido was about to dig in when he suddenly frowned.

The reason was simple. Tohka had brought back barely any food. Even less than appetite-less Shido.

"Tohka?" he said. "Is that going to be enough for you?"

"Mm." She nodded. "Yes. This is all I need for my tummy to be full to bursting."

"…?!" Shido felt a shiver of fear. It wasn't possible. There was just too little on the plate sitting before Tohka. Even a high school girl with a tiny stomach wouldn't be satisfied with these meager offerings. And Tohka was a glutton, far surpassing anyone else Shido knew. That amount of food would never hold her over until supper.

He tapped his earpiece to indicate an emergency. But apparently *Fraxinus* didn't need Shido's report to be unnerved.

"That's… Tohka with that rabbit food?!"

"She can't be sick, can she?!"

"Ridiculous! That bottomless pit?!"

He could hear the cries of the crew and their frantic tapping at their consoles. He thought he could also hear a slightly rude name-calling, perhaps because of the confusion, but he decided to pretend that he hadn't heard that.

Because Tohka's un-Tohka-like behavior hinted at a possibility. Namely, that this was not the real Tohka.

"Reine!" he said.

"...*Calm down*," Reine replied, coolly. "*We'll watch and wait for now.*"

Shido placed a hand on his chest to try and calm his pounding heart and turned back to Tohka. "What's wrong? Are you not feeling well?"

"I'm fine. Why?"

"Why? Well, I mean." He glanced at her plate, but Tohka appeared not to notice.

She clapped her hands. "Anyway, let's eat!"

"R-right. We should eat." Shido began to tuck into the food on his plate.

"That was great," Tohka said gloomily.

"Huh?!" His eyebrows jumped up on his forehead when he looked across the table and saw that Tohka's plate was empty. "Y-you're done already?"

"...Mm-hmm. It was good." Tohka clapped her hands together once more. But she was clearly not satisfied.

"Tohka," he said. "Are you sure you had enough?"

"O-of course I did!" She hurriedly nodded. But in that moment, a puppy bark came from her stomach. *Ruk.*

"Umm. What was that?"

"Th-this is plenty for me."

Grrrr. Ruk ruk ruk.

"Tohka?"

"I-I'm telling you I'm fine!"

Grrr. Grar grar grar grar.

The remarkably loud sounds emanating from her stomach made Tohka hang her head.

"N-ngh!" Shido furrowed his brow, doubtfully. "See? That really isn't enough. What's up with you today?"

Tohka was quiet for a moment and then lifted her face in resignation. "On TV yesterday, they were talking about how a girl who eats too much is a turnoff..."

"Huh?"

"And...I didn't want to be a turnoff for you, Shido, so..." Tohka shrank into herself in embarrassment.

Shido exhaled like it all made sense now. "I actually prefer girls who enjoy eating a whole lot," he told her.

"R-really?!" Her eyes lit up.

"Yeah," he said. "In fact, it makes me sad when food goes unfinished."

Tohka gasped before nodding forcefully and leaping to her feet. She marched over to the buffet area, filled a big plate with as much food as she could cram onto it, and returned. The other diners and the wait staff stared after her in shock.

But Tohka paid them no mind at all. "Time to eat!"

3:15 PM.

"That was the same old Tohka, huh?" Shido muttered to himself back at home, as he recalled the way Tohka had acted, and checked the time on his phone.

After lunch, Shido and Tohka had walked through the town and gotten a bunch of shopping done, chatting the whole time, but he hadn't been able to pick out anything strange about her.

Of course, just as Reine instructed, he'd asked all sorts of leading questions and quizzed her on things that only Tohka could have known. But she had answered all of them quite easily. When he considered all that, it was hard to believe she could have been Natsumi in disguise.

"So then I guess it's actually someone else, huh?" Shido said to his earpiece.

"*...We can't say anything definitive at this point.*" Reine's voice came back to him. "*In any case, all we can do is have faith that Natsumi's* *transformation ability has seams we can pull apart and forge ahead with our investigation. It's almost time. You need to start your second date."*

"Right." He nodded. "Who's next? Where should I go?"

"...*Mm, you can stay right where you are, Shin.*"

"Huh?"

"...*The timing's perfect. She wanted to see you anyway. So I decided you could get two birds with one stone. I think she should be there—*"

Bing bong!

The doorbell interrupted Reine.

"Hmm? Who's that?" Shido glanced at the intercom screen, but there was no one on it. Cocking his head, he went out into the hallway and walked toward the front door to open it.

"Yes? Who is—"

"*Boo!*"

"Gah?!"

The second he turned the doorknob, something flew at him through the crack of an opening, and Shido automatically threw himself backward. The phone in his hand slid out and flew toward the thing that had poked its face into the entryway.

But the thing dodged the phone neatly and crossed tiny arms in indignation.

"*Honestly, Shido! You gotta watch what you're doing!*"

When Shido looked closely, he saw that the thing was a puppet in the shape of a rabbit. Yoshino's friend, Yoshinon. But the puppet had a slightly different look from the Yoshinon that Shido knew.

There were stitches on its face and massive bolts stuck onto its head. It looked almost like a robot.

"Y-Yoshinon," he said. "That *is* you, right?"

"*Yuuuup. Everyone's superstar, Yoshinon, y'know?*" it joked, and Shido let out a sigh of relief. Although it was looking rather eerie, inside was apparently the same old Yoshinon.

As Shido scooped his phone from the floor, the door slowly swung inward, and a girl peered in very timidly through the opening.

Yoshino. Because Shido had been surprised and taken his hand off the knob, only Yoshinon on her left hand had made it inside.

"Oh, and Yoshino, too! Sorry. I was just surprised." He pulled the door open all the way and then jumped again.

Like Yoshinon, Yoshino looked different than usual. She wore a pointed black hat with a broad brim and a jet-black robe. She held a small broom in her right hand. Yes. She was dressed like a witch, the very picture of the Natsumi who Shido was currently in search of.

"Y-Yoshino… What…?" he asked.

Yoshinon poked at Yoshino's cheeks as if to encourage her. *"Come on, come on, Yooooshino."*

"Uh. Uh-huh…!" Yoshino bobbed her head up and down, and then looked at Shido determinedly. "Tr-trick or treat…!"

"Huh?" For a second, Shido gaped at her, but then he quickly realized what she meant and slapped a fist into a hand. "Oh, is that it? Is this a Halloween costume?"

It was indeed that time of year. This all made sense to him now.

"So then, Yoshinon, you dressed up, too?"

"Hee-hee-hee! I'm Frankenstein's monster!" Yoshinon threw its arms out, menacingly. That said, well, with its cute eyes and the soft toe beans, it wasn't the least bit intimidating.

"Reine, when you said she wanted to see me?" he asked, in a low voice.

"…Mm-hmm. Yoshino saw people trick-or-treating on TV and said she wanted to try it."

"I get it." Shido said thoughtfully. Halloween was technically October 31, but to get a taste of the experience, now was just as good as then. Although he was surprised because at a glance this silhouette looked like Natsumi's, but the adorable witch look suited little Yoshino very well.

"Mm." He smiled. "You look cute, Yoshino."

"…!"

Yoshino gasped and hung her head, shyly, and Yoshinon jabbed Shido in the arm.

"Hey, okay! I'm glad you're being nice to Yoshino and all, but aren't you forgetting something?"

"Forgetting?" He frowned. "Oh! The candy? Hang on a minute."

Now that he was thinking about it, he had forgotten a key element. He walked into the kitchen and looked around in the cupboard where they kept the snacks. But in unfortunately poor timing, the cupboard was empty. If he went to Kotori's room, he could probably find a stock of Chupa Chups, but if he touched them, he didn't know what kind of retribution he would face later.

"Aah." Shido returned to the entryway and bowed apologetically. "Sorry. Looks like we're all out of candy right now."

Yoshino's shoulders slumped, dejectedly. "You…are?"

"I'm really sorry. I'll make sure to have some here next—" Shido started, but FrankenYoshinon leaned in close.

"Whoopsy? That's gonna be a real problem, my guy. We're not playing games here. Yoshino! Come on! Do it!"

"H…huh?" she said.

"Ugh. It's trick or treat, okay? If we don't get a treat, we play a trick."

"Oh…" Yoshino looked up at Shido with big, round eyes.

"H-hey?" Shido raised an eyebrow.

"It's just, if you got no treats, we got no choice, Shido. I guess you'll have to enjoy this little prank from Yoshino."

"Pr-prank? What are you going to do?" he asked, taking a step back, and a creepy smile rose up on Yoshinon's face.

"Wait and see." The puppet signaled Yoshino with its eyes. Her cheeks flushed, and she averted her eyes.

"No, seriously. What are you planning to do?!" Shido cried. "Ah! Right. Can you two wait in the living room for a minute?"

"…?"

"Why?"

Yoshino and Yoshinon looked at each other curiously. Beckoning them inside, Shido once again headed for the kitchen.

He pulled the pancake mix out of the cupboard, got some milk and eggs from the fridge, and started measuring things out into a bowl.

"What, what? What are you making, Shidoooo?"

"Wouldn't you like to know? It'll be ready soon, so just wait a minute, okay?" Shido said, and saw the pair cock their heads, eyes round with surprise.

Smiling, he heated a Teflon pan, melted some butter, poured batter in, and neatly fried it. He placed two pancakes on a white plate, buttered them, and drizzled maple syrup to finish them off.

"Okay. It's ready. Eat up while it's still hot," he said, setting the plate down on the table.

Yoshino gaped in surprise and began to scrutinize the pancakes. "I've…seen this on TV…!" She was about to pick up her fork when her shoulders jumped up and she gasped as if remembering something. "Umm… thank you."

"Sure thing. Enjoy," he told her.

Yoshino cut a bite-sized piece of pancake with Yoshinon's help, stabbed a fork into it, and stared at it hard before popping it into her mouth.

"…!"

Her eyes flew open, and she slapped the table repeatedly before giving Shido the thumbs-up. He'd seen her do this before. This was how she reacted when emotionally upended by an unknown flavor. It seemed that she approved.

"Ha-ha! Is it good then?" His face relaxed into a smile.

Yoshino bobbed her head up and down.

"…Shin."

He heard Reine's voice in his right ear.

"…I hate to interrupt this lovely moment, but what do you think? Anything different about Yoshino?"

"Oh. No. From what I can see, I don't think there's anything out of the ordinary," he said, and cleared his throat to get himself back on track. "That reminds me. We did something like this before, too, right? You know. When you first came to the house, Yoshino. Umm, what did I make that time?"

Yoshino and Yoshinon looked at each other before turned back to Shido.

"Yes… That time, you…made us chicken and egg bowls," Yoshino said, an ecstatic look on her face.

Shido smiled at her and said to himself, "Bingo."

"Huh? What's that about, Shido? Yoshinon doesn't know a thing about that," Yoshinon said, unhappily, face covered in stitches.

"Hmm? You don't remember?" he asked.

Yoshinon made a gesture like it was thinking for a second before hitting one hand in its other palm. *"Maybe that was when Yoshinon was at Origami's house?"*

"Oh. Right. I guess you weren't with Yoshino then."

"I wasn't. Still, giving Yoshino a chicken and egg bowl while Yoshinon's out of the picture's pretty pervy, Shido! Trying to go up to that adult level while Yoshinon's not looking, hmm? Wait. If Yoshino's the egg, then who's the chicken?"

"Y-Yoshinon!" A tomato-faced Yoshino pressed a hand over Yoshinon's mouth, and the puppet flailed its arms.

"Mmph! Mmph!"

It wasn't as though the puppet was equipped with lungs, but Yoshinon struggled like it couldn't breathe.

Shido felt bad for it somehow and said to Yoshino, "H-hey. Yoshinon's having a rough time over there."

"Oh… I-I'm sorry, Yoshinon…!" She yanked her hand away.

"Koff! Koff! …*Phew. I thought I was a goner there,*" Yoshinon said, relieved, and then tilted its head curiously.

"Hmm? Is something wrong, Yoshinon?" Shido asked.

Yoshinon crossed its arms deftly and groaned. *"Mm, I forgot. 'Cause of the lack of oxygen from Yoshino pinning me down. Shido, you better be careful when you have a fight with Yoshino, too."*

"Th-that's…" Yoshino flushed red, and then polished off the rest of the pancakes as if to cover up her embarrassment.

After a minute or two, Yoshinon pricked its ears up and whispered something to Yoshino. *"…Okay? …that's why, …you know."*

Yoshino turned her eyes toward Shido, urged on by Yoshinon,

stabbed her fork into the last piece of pancake, and held out her hand in Shido's direction. "Uh. Umm. I'm sharing."

"Oh. But I actually gave that to you, so…," Shido said.

"…"

Yoshino's eyebrows rose up sadly on her forehead.

When she made that face, he couldn't very well refuse. Shido held out his hands to indicate his surrender and then chomped down on the proffered pancake, being careful to keep his mouth off the fork.

Watching this, a bold smile spread across Yoshinon's face. *"Shi-doooo. If Yoshinon's memory is correct, some people eat pancakes as a snack, but there are also people who eat them for breakfast, right?"*

"Huh?" he said. "Oh, well, yeah, I guess so."

"Right? So then isn't it not quite right to call this a treat?"

"Wh-whoa, hey." He didn't need to hear that when the treat in question had already been devoured.

"Umm. Shido." Yoshino timidly pointed at his face. "You have… syrup. On the corner of your mouth."

"Huh? Really?" The piece of pancake must have been a bit larger than bite-sized. Shido licked his lips.

"It's a little more… This way. Oh. Do you mind?" Yoshino said, standing up, and took one of the wet wipes on the table.

"S-sure." He did feel a bit awkward, but she was going out of her way to do him a favor. His face turned red, but he stopped himself from averting his eyes.

When Yoshino reached toward his face, however, she kept going and brought her own face in close before licking a spot somewhere between his cheek and his lip.

"Waah?!" He jumped up and flew backward. That was indeed unexpected. "Y-Y-Y-Y-Y-Yoshino?!"

"Uh. Umm. Umm. Uh…" For some reason, she was just as flustered as he was. She stammered and flapped her hands. "Th-that was… Umm. Pancakes are kind of. In between dinner and a treat, so… I-I played a trick…!" she cried out and ran out of the house.

Shido was momentarily stunned, and then he spoke to his earpiece. "R-Reine... That was really Yoshino...right?"

"...*Hmm, good question.*"

The response he got was noncommittal.

◇

"Umm. So then who's next?" Shido asked his earpiece.

A couple seconds later, Reine replied, "*...Mm-hmm. Next is Hiroto Tonomachi.*"

"Tonomachi?" Shido said, with a sigh of relief. Tonomachi had been his friend for ages and was also the lone boy in the group of suspects. This investigation was maybe less of a date and more hanging out.

"*...You sound happy about that.*"

"Ha-ha-ha! Well, Tonomachi's a boy and everything. It might just be easier is all."

"*...Mm. That's great then. We might be able to finish this one faster. A text has already been sent to him in your name. You're scheduled to meet in an hour.*"

"Got it. Where are we meeting?"

"*...Oh, that's—*"

Shido's face paled when she told him.

About an hour later, Shido and Tonomachi were sitting next to each other on a sauna bench.

Yes. The meeting place Ratatoskr had specified was in front of the large-scale spa in the neighborhood.

" "

...

" "

...

They had sat down next to each other a few minutes earlier, but they hadn't spoken at all. Even though Shido hung out with Tonomachi all the time, he was more nervous than on a date with a girl. The whole thing was just too awkward.

"H-hey. Tonomachi?" he said, at last, unable to stand the silence, and Tonomachi's shoulders jerked up.

"…! Wh-what's up, Itsuka?"

"Oh…Just like… Sorry." Shido bowed slightly and turned away from his friend. "Reine, why did you pick a place like this?!"

"*…It's two guys at last. I thought it would be nice if you could spend some quality time naked together.*" The high-performance, precision-manufactured Ratatoskr earpiece transmitted Reine's sleepy voice with a clear quality even in the extremely hot and humid sauna.

"What is that absurd logic? And like, the timing is so completely wrong. I don't know exactly what happened, but I do know that Natsumi said something to Tonomachi when she was pretending to be me. I feel like he's being super cold, or like on guard or something."

"*…If he was hostile toward you, he wouldn't have accepted the invitation to start with.*"

"I'm not talking hostility. It's more like he thinks I've got some wild kinks or something. Or like he's got some weird ideas about me." As he spoke, Shido glanced over at Tonomachi. He was sure that his friend's cheeks were red only because of the heat in the sauna. Obviously.

"*…And there is actual meaning in the selection of that place.*" Reine continued, quietly. "*Natsumi's a woman. She no doubt has some resistance to being naked with a man, regardless of whether she's transformed or not.*"

"Oh." He nodded. "That actually makes sense."

Reine might have been exactly right. If Tonomachi were Natsumi, she would have come up with some reason to decline an invitation to the spa.

"So then, the fact that he's here means that Tonomachi isn't Natsumi?"

"*…I think it's a strong possibility. Although, well, we can't rule out the possibility that Natsumi has the sort of kink where she gets excited showing off her own private parts.*"

"…"

Shido remained silent. Well, it was true that if that were the case, this wouldn't be much of a reference point.

"So then what should I do? I guess asking about stuff from way back that Natsumi wouldn't know is the reasonable thing?"

"...*Yes, that's fundamental. I'd also like to see his reaction and numbers for one other thing. Could you touch him a little?*"

"Huh?" Shido's pupils shrank into stunned dots.

Reine continued, evenly. "...*Even if Natsumi has no issue with exposing her naked body, as I mentioned, she should still react if that body is abruptly touched.*"

"Uh... Uh-huh." Shido swallowed to wet a throat dry with the heat and nerves, and turned back to Tonomachi.

At the same time, Tonomachi opened his mouth. "H-hey, Itsuka. Why'd you ask me to a place like this today?"

"Huh? Oh. Th-the thing is..."

"...*Shin, now.*"

The order from Reine came in while Shido was fumbling for an answer.

Although he was confused, he followed her instruction, reached out a hand, and touched Tonomachi like he was going to throw an arm over his shoulders.

"Eeep?!" Tonomachi jumped and scooted to the side, like he was fleeing. When Shido looked closely, he could see goosebumps on his friend's body. "Wh-wh-wh-wh-wh-wh-wh-wh-wh-what are you doing, Itsuka?!"

"Oh. Uh... Hey."

"..."

"..."

An uncomfortable silence fell once more.

Shido shielded his right ear from Tonomachi and tapped his earpiece. "So? How was his reaction?"

"...*Mm. He was relatively flustered. The moment you touched him, his tension values leaped way up.*"

"Huh? So then...?"

"*...I want a little more data. Try touching him a few more times.*"

"Uh. Uh-huh..." He was deeply reluctant to do that, but this too was in the service of identifying Natsumi. Shido stood up from the bench and then sat back down next to Tonomachi. When he did, Tonomachi's shoulders shuddered again.

"I-Itsuka... We're friends...right? Just regular friends."

"Mm. Uh-huh," Shido said. "We are."

"—! Right! Ha. Ha-ha." Tonomachi laughed weakly. "Aah, sorry, my bad. I kinda got the wrong—"

"Yup." Shido plopped a hand down on Tonomachi's thigh.

"Eeegyaaaah?!" Tonomachi shrieked and darted out of the sauna.

"Aah." Shido sighed softly as he walked alone down the road. He'd had a nice soak in the bath, but that hadn't taken the edge off of his exhaustion. In fact, he even felt like he was more exhausted than he'd been before he got in. But he didn't have the luxury of wallowing. He still had one last person to meet for that day's quota. "Umm, we're meeting at the park on the hill, right?"

"*...Yes. You're a little late. Hurry it up.*"

"Okay!" Shido quickened his pace and hurried to the meeting spot. Now that the sun had set, the air was cool on his skin, perfect for after he'd warmed himself up in the bath.

He reached the park soon enough. A girl was already there, in front of the bench illuminated by a streetlamp. Glamorous in a patterned, long-sleeved blouse and a flared black skirt. One half of the Yamai sisters—Yuzuru Yamai.

"Outrage. You have quite the nerve to ask someone out and then be late," Yuzuru said, glaring at him from under half-lidded eyes.

Shido hurriedly ran over to her, clasped his hands together, and bowed. Well, to be precise, it hadn't been Shido who asked her out, but rather Reine and Ratatoskr. Yuzuru had no way of knowing that, however. "Sorry, Yuzuru. The thing I was doing before went long."

"Amnesty. Well, that's fine. Yuzuru is generous of heart, so I will give you a margin of error of five minutes," she said, and then sighed and crossed her arms.

Shido ran his hand through his hair, feeling that something was off somehow. It wasn't that he had any issue with Yuzuru's behavior. If he had to say, it might just have been the effect of the oddity of there being only one of the Yamai sisters when he was used to seeing two. It was no exaggeration to say that since Shido had sealed their Spirit powers, the sisters were always together except when they went to the washroom.

As if guessing at this line of thought from his gaze, Yuzuru shrugged, exasperated. "Sigh. Is Yuzuru alone insufficient?"

"No, it's not that at all. I was just thinking it was a little bit strange," he told her.

"Negation. There is no need for you to be delicate. Yuzuru and Kaguya are two hearts beating as one. In fact, your reaction is proof that Yuzuru and Kaguya are bound together." She grinned boldly. It seemed that the two Yamais were close even now. "Question. What is going on that you would ask me out at this hour?"

"Oh, well, I just wanted to talk a bit, just the two of us," he told her. "Is that not allowed?"

Her eyes grew round in surprise. "Negation. It's not *not* allowed. But if that's the case…" She smiled, took his arm, and pulled herself in close. Her ample bust pressed against his arm.

"Y-Yuzuru?" he stammered.

"Monopoly. Tonight alone, you belong to Yuzuru. And tonight alone, Yuzuru belongs to you. Isn't that right?" she said, her sweet breath tickling his neck.

He unconsciously blushed at her bewitching manner, so unlike how she normally cavorted with Kaguya.

"Suggestion. Would you like to walk a bit, Shido?"

"Huh?" He cocked his head, and Yuzuru giggled and pulled him along.

They walked around the outskirts of the park at a leisurely pace. High up on the hill as it was, the place had a view of the whole of Tengu, the city where Shido and his friends lived. The electrical lights twinkled like stars in the dark streets.

"Wonder. It's so beautiful."

"Yeah. It really is," Shido replied, honestly, and Yuzuru looked at his face, with half-lidded eyes. "Wh-what?"

"Point. When a woman says 'it's beautiful,' it is considered appropriate for the man to reply, 'You are more beautiful.'"

"...Is that how it goes?"

"Assent. That is how it goes." Yuzuru said, seeming full of confidence.

Where had she picked up this knowledge? Shido smiled, wryly. "Y-you're...more beautiful."

"Smile. Hee hee! Am I really?" Her cheeks flushed slightly, a small smile on her lips.

His heart automatically started to beat faster at the adorable look on her face. He didn't get to see too much of it in everyday life.

He couldn't really relax, though.

Even after a Spirit's powers were sealed, they could flow back if her mood became unstable. Thus, Shido often found himself soothing Tohka. But because the mental states of the Yamai sisters were extremely stable as long as they were together, he hadn't really had to do much heavy lifting with these Spirits. In fact, while Tohka had been put into the same class as Shido, the Yamai sisters were in the class next to his. To be frank, he felt more of a sense of friendship with the Yamai sisters than he did with Tohka or Yoshino.

But—no, actually, because of that, it was quite novel to be speaking with Yuzuru alone like this, and he found himself a little overwrought.

"Hail. Shido?" she said, softly.

"Hmm? What?" he replied.

Yuzuru cleared her throat before continuing. "Petition. Please answer honestly."

"O-okay. So what is it?"

"Question. Who do you prefer, Shido? Yuzuru or Kaguya?"

"Huh?" He stared, stunned by the unexpected question. He awkwardly stammered, "Wh-why would you…?"

Yuzuru's intent stare did not waver. She didn't look like she was making a joke or fooling around.

"I-I can't just choose one of you. I care for both of you," he told her.

Yuzuru shrugged in resignation. "Sneer. My goodness. So you chose the weakest, most pathetic response, hmm?"

"Sh-shut up!" he cried. "You can't just up and ask me something like that out of nowhere and expect me to answer!"

"Confirmation. Then if I give you a preparation period, will you answer me properly?"

"Ungh…!" He was at a loss for words.

Yuzuru sighed again.

Shido thought about it a bit. "So you wanted me to choose one of you."

"Consideration. I suppose." Yuzuru put a finger to her chin as if thinking this over. And then she turned her gaze on Shido once more. "Answer. If you choose Kaguya, then I will praise you and tell you that you are good and smart. If you choose Yuzuru, I will flip." She smiled mischievously.

Kaguya and Yuzuru were like that. They each love-love-loved the other more than their own selves.

"Good to know," he said, with a sigh.

"Addition. But if you choose Yuzuru…I would be happy."

"Huh?" Shido felt his heart pound even harder. And glued to his side the way she was, Yuzuru might have also noticed this. He shook his head vigorously, and tried to distract her from the thumping of his heart. "Wh-which is it then?"

"Sigh. It's just as I said. I don't mind either way. But that chicken answer. I'm disappointed in you. Useless."

"Hngh…" He couldn't say anything in response to that.

Yuzuru paid this no mind. "But," she added. "Petition. If. This is an

if. If Kaguya asks you the same question as Yuzuru just now…please make sure you reply 'Kaguya.'"

"Huh? That's…" He didn't know what to say.

"Prediction. Kaguya will definitely be angry. Something like, 'Why didn't you choose Yuzuru!' But in her heart, she will be unbearably happy."

"Yuzuru…"

"Conviction. Kaguya is normally like *that*, but she adores you, Shido. I'm telling you this, so there's no mistake. Yuzuru and Kaguya were originally one. The things Yuzuru hates, Kaguya also hates. In the same way, the things Yuzuru likes, Kaguya loves."

"Uh. That's…" His eyebrows jumped up, and Yuzuru eyes widened a bit.

She put a hand to her mouth and pulled away from Shido. "Careless. That was extra information. I will depart before I say any other unnecessary things."

"H-hey, Yuzuru?!" Shido called.

Yuzuru looked back with a smile. "Petition. I was not lying. Kaguya likes you very much, Shido. So please. Take good care of her."

She bowed and ran off into the night.

"…And you let her just go alone like that? Aaah. You could have at least seen her back to the apartment building." Kotori lay back on the sofa as she let out an exasperated sigh.

Shido, Kotori, and Reine were currently in the Itsuka living room. Shido had been made to sit on the floor, while Kotori was on the sofa in front of him, and Reine was sitting on the sofa to one side, watching over the two of them.

After he'd been abandoned in the park, Shido had nothing else to do but return home, and when he did, Kotori and Reine were standing by already in the living room. Lecture time started pretty much immediately.

"Making a girl walk home alone at night, that's not a choice I can respect too much."

"Ngh... I'm sorry."

Now that she mentioned it, that was exactly right. But Yuzuru had raced down the hill so fast while Shido stood there baffled. As expected of a wind Spirit. There was no way he could have caught up with her.

"...Well, he didn't have much of a choice given the situation. You did good, Shin." Reine threw out a life raft for him. She knew what happened. She had watched from *Fraxinus*.

Kotori snorted and flicked the stick of her Chupa Chups. "I know. I mean, I get that this is a lot to cram into one day." She looked at Shido. "So. You talked to four people today. You notice anything weird? Tohka, Yoshino, Tonomachi, Yuzuru. Any of them seem like they could be Natsumi?"

"..."

Shido went over the day's events in his mind.

He had only investigated a third of the suspects. And it was true that if he wanted to suspect one of them, he could have found a reason to. But he couldn't say at the moment that any one of them was the culprit.

"I still don't know," he said, finally. "Anyway, I need to check everyone first."

"Well...I guess so." Kotori had apparently anticipated that response. She rolled her eyes and sighed. "I'm checking all the recordings myself, so I'll tell you if I catch anything."

"Okay. Thanks."

"Well, anyway. Call it a day here," she said, recrossing her legs. "You've got more to deal with tomorrow. I don't need your morning plans getting all messed up because of a lack of sleep."

Shido stood up. "Yeah, okay. I'll do that then. Reine, what time do I start tomorrow?"

"...Mm. Your first date is at ten. Sorry, but you'll have to skip school."

"It is what it is," he said, resigned to his fate. "We're on a deadline, after all. Umm, my first date is..."

"...With Kotori."

"...!"

Reclining on the sofa, Kotori twitched.

Reine clapped her hands like she'd just realized something. "...Oh, right. I meant to tell you not to oversleep tomorrow."

"—! Y—! That's not the issue here! As commander I was simply...!" Kotori threw a cushion at Shido when he turned his gaze on her.

"Whoa! Hey!" he protested. "What are you doing?!"

"Shut up! Just go to bed already!" she shouted, and grabbed another cushion.

Shido quickly retreated to his room.

The minute and second hands of the clock moved with a loud *tic* and pointed at 12:00 at the same time.

Twelve AM. The end of October 22 and the start of the 23rd. In other words, the first day of the *game* was over.

"Hee hee!" Natsumi, transformed into *someone*, giggled quietly in the darkness.

Shido hadn't been able to guess who Natsumi was on this first day. That didn't surprise her, though. There were over ten suspects, and the rules she'd set were ambiguous. There wasn't much he could have done on the first day.

Regardless, however, the first day of the game was over.

"Haniel. It's time," Natsumi said, too quietly for anyone else to hear, and snapped her fingers. That was all she had to do. Haniel would take care of the rest, just as she desired.

"Now then... First one person. Will you actually be able to guess who I am?"

More giggles.

The witch laughed.

"Before anyone disappears."

"Nn…"

Morning. Hearing a noise, Shido stretched in his bed and rubbed his eyes. Yawning widely, he reached a hand out and pressed the button on his alarm clock.

But the noise didn't stop. Whatever it was that had disturbed his sleep, it was not his alarm clock.

"Huh?" He sat up slowly and yawned again. As his mind gradually woke up, he grasped the true nature of the noise. Yes, it was…the doorbell. The doorbell of the Itsuka house was ringing incessantly.

"What's going on? First thing in the morning…" Grumbling, he got out of bed, plodded down the stairs, and walked down the hallway, the doorbell ringing the whole time.

But when he reached the entryway, the mysterious caller apparently grew tired of waiting. They came through the gate and began making the doorknob clack back and forth.

"Whoa?!"

It was one thing first thing in the morning, but this would have been pure horror at night.

"Wh-who is it?" he called out very tentatively.

"Shido!"

He heard a girl's frantic voice from the other side of the door. A familiar, high-pitched voice—Kaguya.

"Kaguya? What on earth—?" He unlocked the door, and Kaguya came flying in, her forehead damp with perspiration. "Whoa! Hey! Calm down! What happened?!"

"Sh-Shido! Is Yuzuru here?!" she shouted, apparently forgetting about her usual arrogant manner of speaking.

"Yuzuru?" Shido tilted his head dubiously. "No, she's not here… Why?"

"Sh-she's gone… When I woke up this morning, Yuzuru was totally gone!" Kaguya half-shrieked.

"What?!" Shido cried, furrowing his brow.

Maybe *this* moment was the true start of Natsumi's game.

Chapter 4
High Risk

"..."
"..."

Sitting side by side on the park bench, Shido and Kotori stared at the fountain in silence.

Actually, to be more precise, they weren't looking at it. It was simply that there happened to be a fountain in front of them. Shido was hunched over, his elbows propped up on his knees, while Kotori had her legs crossed and was leaning back against the bench, both of them in quiet contemplation.

The time was 11:30 AM. The park was full of housewives with children and old folks taking walks. Perhaps the young boy and girl sitting wordlessly on a bench in the middle of this drew attention; Shido got the feeling that the mothers were glancing at them from time to time.

Neither of them had the presence of mind to pay these busybodies any attention at the moment. This was only natural, of course. Because Yuzuru Yamai had disappeared that morning.

After they had been sitting there like that for who knew how long, Kotori abruptly spoke. "Hey, say something. This is supposed to be a date, after all."

"O-oh. Right." Shido let out a short sigh, and clenched his jaw to get himself back on track.

Although it was a little later than initially planned, Shido and Kotori were on a date. It was basically all they could do for the time being.

"Uh... Mm..." But no matter how he tried to come up with something to say, no words came to mind.

Kotori sighed, with annoyance. "You're kind of out of it, huh? Well, I guess you would be."

"Sorry." Shido tousled his own hair and exhaled the frustration and helplessness coiled in his lungs. Naturally, this did almost nothing to clear either of these feelings from his system, however.

With a grimace, Shido recalled the video he'd seen on *Fraxinus* earlier.

Going back in time to ten o'clock.

Reine had come to the Itsuka house. She knew all about Yuzuru's disappearance, but because it seemed best not to tell Kaguya, she, Tohka, and Yoshino were on standby in a room in the neighboring apartment building.

"So then, Reine, where exactly did Yuzuru disappear?" Shido asked.

Reine nodded a little. "...I'll go through it from the start. First, Kaguya says she saw Yuzuru come home to the apartment last night. There's no mistake there?"

"No. That's definitely what she said," Shido said, remembering what Kaguya had told him earlier. She had seen Yuzuru come home the previous evening. Yuzuru had been tired maybe, so they hadn't talked much, but Kaguya saw her go into the bath and then get into bed.

Meaning Yuzuru disappeared in the few hours between evening and morning.

"...Take a look at this." Reine set out a terminal on the table. A video of what looked to be an apartment was shown on the small monitor.

He knew this place. This was the bedroom of the apartment where Kaguya and Yuzuru lived together. Two beds had identical girls sleeping in them.

"You record this kind of thing?" he asked, looking up at Reine.

"...Mm-hmm. And not just the Yamais' apartment. Autonomous

cameras have been deployed to the rooms of all the Natsumi suspects. I thought we might be able to get a lead on this thing when no one was watching."

Reine tapped at her console once more. The video of the Yamai sisters began to play on fast-forward. The hands on the clock in the room spun around, and the girls tossed and turned at a hectic pace.

"…Right about now," Reine said, pushed a key, and the playback speed returned to normal.

Soon, the hands of the clock indicated 12:00 AM.

"Wha…?"

"What is this…?"

Kotori and Shido said, at the same time.

The center of the bedroom appeared to twist on the monitor, and something like a broom appeared out of thin air.

"Is that…Haniel?" he asked.

Yes. It was Natsumi's Angel Haniel, the broom he'd seen a few days earlier.

Haniel slowly opened up to expose a mirror-like interior. And then that mirror flashed. The body of Yuzuru in her bed shone faintly before it was sucked into the mirror.

"…! Yuzuru!" Of course, this was all happening in a video. Shido's cry was in vain, and the girl disappeared without a trace.

And then, having sucked Yuzuru in, Haniel slowly closed up again and melted into the air.

"…It's just as you saw." Reine twirled her chair around to face Shido. "Yuzuru was abducted by Natsumi's Angel Haniel. Most likely, the real person Natsumi's impersonating was made to disappear the same way."

"I-Is Yuzuru okay?! And what about whoever Natsumi's impersonating?!" Shido cried.

Reine lowered her eyes, troubled. "…I want to believe they're okay, but I can't say anything at the present time."

Not knowing what to do with all the frustration and anger swirling around in his heart, Shido tore at his hair. "What exactly am I supposed to do here?!"

"…There's one thing you can do. Find Natsumi among the suspects as soon as possible."

"That's exactly it." Kotori pulled the Chupa Chups she was sucking on out of her mouth and snapped it at Shido. "No time to waste. Let's start our date."

Back to the present, East Tengu Park.

While Shido was remembering what happened on *Fraxinus*, Kotori stood up, took a few steps, and struck a daunting pose between Shido and the fountain.

"Kotori?" He frowned.

"Hup!" Kotori threw a sharp chop at the top of his head.

"Ow!" he cried. "Wh-what are you doing?!"

"Quit with the doom and gloom," she said. "You think moping's going to bring Yuzuru back?"

"I-I just…!" Shido started, and then shook his head, rethinking himself. "Ah, you're totally right, Kotori. I shouldn't be doing that now."

Kotori snorted as she flicked up the stick of the Chupa Chups in her mouth. "So long as you get it. And all the more so now that Natsumi's gone and added rules without telling us. Actually, it's not so much added. I suppose it's more like she finally revealed the details?" She scowled, annoyed.

Rules with details revealed. That was without a doubt the phenomenon that happened with Yuzuru the night before.

"'Before anyone disappears,'" he said. "So this is what that last line on the card meant, huh?"

"Probably. This is just my hypothesis, but it's likely that Haniel will take one of the suspects each day that passes. And then once they're all gone—except for whoever Natsumi's impersonating—she wins. If we can find her before that happens, though, it's your win, Shido." Kotori held up a finger as she outlined her thoughts.

Indeed, if they took the sentence on the card Natsumi sent at face value, then that is how it would go.

"I wonder if I can actually find her," he said, finally.

"I don't want to hear your whining," Kotori replied. "Now that Yuzuru's gone, there are eleven suspects, including me. You've only got ten more days."

"Oh. Right." Shido nodded, firmly.

And then they were silent again.

Kotori spoke up, impatiently. "And Shido?"

"Hmm? What is it?"

"You've only got half an hour left before your next appointment."

"Huh? Oh, right," he replied, vaguely, and her mouth twisted downward.

"So I'm saying you maybe need to investigate me," she told him.

"Oh…" His eyes opened wide. He'd forgotten until that very second, but Kotori might also have been Natsumi in disguise.

Naturally, he didn't want to suspect the adorable little sister who had lit a fire under him just now and given him encouragement. But if the fake was Kotori, Ratatoskr commander, the damage would be much greater than with anyone else. For the future, too, he had to prove her innocence.

"You're right." He nodded. "Okay, I'll ask you some questions."

She raised an eyebrow at him. "Here?"

"Huh?"

"It is just a pretext for the investigation, but this is still a date, you know," she reminded him.

Shido fussed awkwardly. "Oh."

Her words made him remember the conversation between Kotori and Reine the previous day.

They might have been at wit's end faced with Yuzuru's disappearance, but this was a date. Just because it was with Kotori who happened to know what was actually going on didn't mean that he could simply ask her some business-like questions and be done with it.

He exhaled softly, stood up from the bench, and held out a hand. "Right. How about we walk a bit?"

"Mm." Kotori looked a bit dejected, but her cheeks blushed slightly as she took his hand and stood.

And then, holding hands, they began to walk slowly around the edge of the park.

"I feel like it's been ages since we walked just the two of us like this, huh?" he said.

"Mm." She shrugged. "I guess."

"So I'll ask anyway. You remember where we went on our date in June?"

"Of course I do. Ocean Park."

"Ha-ha! Correct."

Kotori sniffed, indignantly. "But if I were Natsumi, there maybe wouldn't be much point to a question like that."

"Huh?" He frowned. "What do you mean?"

"Think about it. I might be prohibited from boarding *Fraxinus*, but I know the general gist of the investigation. It'd only make sense that I would have looked up past stuff," Kotori said, the corners of her mouth turning up smartly.

Shido started to sweat a bit. "H-hey, hey. Quit with the jokes."

"I wish it was a joke. At any rate, you know… You need to investigate using a method that doesn't depend on stuff like that. Don't you?" For some reason, Kotori averted her eyes.

He looked down at her. "What kind of method?"

"This is just a for instance, but to check her reaction, you could try…" Kotori trailed off.

"Try? What?" he pressed her.

"Y-you know." She looked away, awkwardly. "Come on. That. You know… K… K…"

"Oh." He suddenly realized what she was trying to say, and his shoulders jumped up.

Fortunately, he had an idea about this particular method.

"Kotori, could you close your eyes a sec?"

"—! Oh… O-okay…" Kotori blushed slightly as she lowered her eyes.

"Hup!" He brought his hands to either side of her face, and yanked off the black ribbons holding her hair up.

"F-fwah?!" Kotori cried out, stunned, perhaps realizing something was off when she felt her freed hair touching her shoulders.

She hurriedly patted her head and found that her ribbons were gone. "A-aaaaah?!"

Tearing up, she lunged at Shido.

"Sh-Shido! What're you doing?! Give them back! Give me my ribbons!" Kotori shouted, as she jumped up and down trying to take back the ribbons Shido held. It was a far cry from the authoritative commander of moments ago.

Kotori had to maintain a strong persona on a daily basis. When she was wearing those black ribbons, she was able to act with confidence and decisiveness. Conversely, when she removed her ribbons, or when she was wearing white ribbons, she switched to innocent and adorable baby sister mode.

In other words, this.

"Shidooooo! Shidooooooo!"

"…"

He'd gotten his confirmation, but maybe because he hadn't seen White Mode Kotori lately, he found this Kotori bouncing like a bunny strangely cute, to the point where he could hardly stand it. He dangled the ribbons before her and pulled his hand up every time she jumped toward them.

"*Sniffle*...ngh..."

At first, she tried desperately to get her ribbons back, but at last, her face crumpled and tears began to form.

"S-sorry. I'm sorry. Here, Kotori."

He had maybe gone a little too far. He handed the ribbons over, and Kotori snatched them away at lightning speed and tied her hair up on either side of her head.

And then she sloooowly lifted her face and looked at him with a sharp glint in her eyes. "Shido... You..."

"N-no! It's good, we're all good. L-looks like you're the real thing, Kotori!" He raised his voice to emphasize the fact that this had only been a means of testing if she was the genuine article. But she appeared not to even hear him. "K-Kotori? Just calm down—"

"Shut iiiiiiiiit!" Kotori's right fist slammed straight into Shido's face, with a masterful twist added to it.

"Shido. Your face is somewhat…"

After his date with Kotori, he headed toward his next appointment, and Kaguya, waiting for him there, took one look at his face and raised her brow skeptically.

But perhaps that was only to be expected. After receiving Kotori's merciless repayment, Shido was left with a cheek that was swollen and bright red, and he had a tissue stuffed up his nose to stop the blood gushing from his nostrils. At the very least, this was not a face that anyone wanted to see on a date.

"Oh," he said. "I was kind of attacked by a boxer on my way here."

"Y-you were…?" Kaguya's face said she clearly didn't believe him, but perhaps because she had more or less guessed at the truth, she didn't push him any further.

She was wearing a shirt with a design of English letters, crosses, skulls, and more all crammed together, and a skirt with plenty of accessories—chains and belts—the so-called Gothic Punk style. When Reine took her shopping for necessities and clothes, she had apparently fallen instantly in love with this outfit and purchased it immediately.

"Hmph. Well, the incident this morning was a surprise. If you're going to investigate, then it is best to petition for the investigation in advance." Kaguya made a point of striking a pose and then pushed her bangs back. There were no traces of the girl who come crying to him in a panic that morning.

Reine had told her later that Yuzuru was at Ratatoskr headquarters for the investigation. It was a fairly flimsy explanation, but it seemed that Kaguya bought it.

"Huh," Shido said, in a quiet voice. "Kaguya seems to be taking this better than I was expecting."

"*...I hope so.*" Reine's troubled voice came in return through his earpiece.

"Huh?" He was about to ask a question in response, but Kaguya cut in, sounding plenty dissatisfied.

"Oi, are you listening to me, Shido? Failure to listen to me is blasphemy. All such misguided fellows shall burn in the fires of hell, fall to the depths of the abyss."

"Oh. Sorry," he said. "I'll make sure to be careful going forward."

"Indeed. See that you do." She sniffed, imperiously. "But how long will this examination of Yuzuru, or what have you, continue?"

"Huh? O-oh. We're talking head office here, so probably ten days or so."

Ten days. That was the currently assumed time limit for Natsumi's game.

Now that he was thinking about it, the idea of doing whatever it took to find Natsumi before the time limit and rescue Yuzuru had maybe been an unconscious declaration of his resolution.

"Hmm." Kaguya twisted up her face, looking bored. But she quickly cleared her throat and looked at Shido again, striking a determined pose. "Keh-keh! Quite the leisurely situation then. Pray earnestly that I do not grow tired of it."

"Right. I'll make sure to ask them to finish up as soon as possible."

"Mm. A just cause. Now, Shido." Kaguya turned neatly on the spot and pointed at the white building behind her. A massive bowling pin towered above them on its roof.

Yes. The place Ratatoskr had designated for his date with Kaguya was a bowling alley a fifteen-minute walk from Tengu Station.

"I did wonder about the suddenness of your request," she told him. "But it seems that you wish to have a contest with me, yes?"

"Oh, it's not really that I want to have a contest," he replied, vaguely.

But Kaguya was apparently not listening to him. "Keh-keh! I commend your courage, but perhaps it extends into the realm of foolhardy. I am a child of the hurricane, Kaguya Yamai! You have not even the most tenuous chance of victory!"

She took on yet another curiously cool pose. Even against someone other than Yuzuru, her spirit of competition was apparently alive and well.

Well, if it would distract her even a little from the sadness of Yuzuru not being there, then he didn't mind. Shido emitted a short sigh and stepped into the bowling alley with her.

They rented shoes and balls at the counter, and were about to walk over to the lane they'd been given when Kaguya tugged on the hem of his shirt.

"H-halt, Shido. Look there." She pointed across the counter, eyes shining strangely.

Shido craned his neck in that direction.

There was a small area with all kinds of bowling merchandise set out for sale. Shoes and balls like the ones Shido and Kaguya had just rented, a bag to put them in, and other things were displayed in a showcase. He started to say that they were fine with the rentals, but he soon understood why Kaguya was pointing at the showcase.

Next to the balls were the extremely cool gloves that pro bowlers often wore on their dominant hand. And it seemed that they were not available to rent.

"Okay, you win." Shido let out a short sigh, turned to the sales counter, bought a woman's glove, and handed it to Kaguya. "Here. Try it on."

"O-oooh!" Her cheeks flushed with excitement, and she quickly slid her hand into the glove. "This is the legendary Fegefeur Gauntlet!"

"Is it legendary...?"

"Keh-keh! Do you hear me, Shido? Offer up this divine instrument to mine hand. The contest before us begins with an even greater gap now, hmm?" She held up the arm with the gloved hand before happily changing into her bowling shoes and running toward the lane.

Shrugging in exasperation, Shido trailed after her.

"Now then, shall we begin? I cede to you the first throw as a special privilege. Keh-keh! Squirm and struggle!"

"Yeah, yeah..." Shido picked up his ball and was about to walk over to the lane with the pins neatly lined up when Kaguya called out to him.

"Halt! I have had an excellent idea."

"Hmm?" He raised an eyebrow at her. "What is it?"

"A mere contest lacks intrigue," she declared. "Let us make a small wager. How about the loser must do whatever the victor asks?"

"Umm. Where'd that idea come from?" Shido screwed up his face in distaste, and Kaguya smiled boldly, covering half of her face in a very cool move with the hand in the glove.

"Keh-keh! What? Do you suddenly fear losing?"

"No, it's not the losing. I'm more worried about what you'll—" Shido started to say, and then he heard Reine's voice in his right ear.

"*...Well, it's probably fine. If it's some unthinkable demand, we'll put a stop to it.*"

"..."

Shido sighed and turned back to Kaguya. "Fine. But if you're going to have us bet, then I'm going to play for real."

Kaguya grinned, happily. "Kah-kah-kah! Now the game becomes interesting! Excellent. I shall see this 'for real' of yours! Make me yield!"

"Okay then. Just watch." Shido sharpened his gaze and threw the ball with beautiful form.

The reddish-purple, thirteen-pound ball rolled straight down the lane and burst through the center of the pins' V-formation. They toppled like dominos with a sharp satisfying noise, and a mark indicating a strike was displayed on the LCD screen hanging above the alley.

"Yes!" he cried. "How d'you like that!"

"Oh-ho! You perform rather well! It wouldn't be interesting if you couldn't!"

"Heh-heh. I go bowling with Tonomachi and the guys sometimes. I'm not going to just lie down and let you beat me." Shido crossed his arms, smugly.

But Kaguya didn't look the least bit flustered as she picked up her orange ball and slowly walked over to the lane.

"Keh-keh! You would do well to watch the whirlwind of a child of the hurricane. And understand how truly powerless you are!"

She swung the hand holding the ball.

"Special strike! Dunkelheit Windhose!!" Shouting the name of a mysterious technique, she slammed the ball into the lane.

Krrnk! Tremors ran through area.

"Hey, whoa! Kaguya! Do you know how to bowl—" Shido sighed in exasperation and then cut himself off.

The ball she'd thrown onto the floor squealed like the tires of a truck accelerating abruptly and started to shoot forward. He didn't know what she had done, but it seemed she'd managed to put a decent amount of spin on it.

The ball charged down the lane, smoke rising up behind it, and easily knocked flying the pins up ahead. And the pins that danced up into the air knocked over all the pins in the adjacent lanes.

A strike mark appeared on the LCD screens in all three lanes at the same time.

"Behold! My special strike, Dunkelheit Windhose!"

"You can't be serious?! Hey!"

"Kah-kah! Yuzuru and I held our own contest some time ago in a diversion such as this! I shall give you a private viewing of all the special strikes I honed and polished at that time!" Kaguya whirled around to face Shido, a determined smile on her face.

An hour or so later, Shido had been completely and utterly defeated.

Although he had somehow succeeded in stopping Kaguya from adding to her point total the strikes in the neighboring lanes, that was really nothing more than empty consolation. His score definitely wasn't bad, but with Kaguya deploying one special strike after the other, by the time the game was half over, the gap between them had grown so large there was no coming back for him.

"Keh-keh! The victory appears to be mine! Well, I will commend you on a battle well fought!"

"…I'm honored," Shido said, holding up both hands to indicate his surrender.

Kaguya nodded, full of self-satisfaction, crossed her arms, and smiled boldly. "Now then. You haven't forgotten, hmm? The promise we exchanged before our sacred battle!"

"I remember it just fine. So? What are you going to make me do?" he asked, and Kaguya's face abruptly grew serious.

She whirled her head around, checking out the area.

"Hmm?" He frowned. "What's wrong?"

"The flow of qi is poor here due to the skein of the ley lines. We relocate." Kaguya took Shido's hand and began walking.

"H-hey!" he protested. "Where are we going?"

"Will you not be silent and come? Ah, perfect. Over there." Kaguya pointed to the break space with its group of vending machines. At a bench behind the machines toward the very back. "We shall sit there."

"Uh. Okay." Shido was uneasy, not knowing what Kaguya was thinking, but he had no right to refuse her at that moment. He quietly did as he was told and sat on the bench.

Without a word, Kaguya sat next to him. Suddenly very serious, she said, quietly, "Now then, I command you. You'd do well to open your heart."

"Wh-what?" He frowned, apprehensively.

Kaguya continued, staring into his eyes. "Swear to me that for the next ten minutes, you will not be surprised, nor flustered, nor refuse me at all whatever I might say. Further swear that you will speak of what happens during that time to absolutely no one."

"Huh…?"

"Swear it!" she pressed him, and Shido automatically nodded at her ghastly force.

"O-okay…"

"Excellent." Kaguya nodded to herself, and didn't say anything for a few moments. Then she abruptly fell into Shido and put her head on his lap.

"…?!"

He nearly cried out at the sudden act, but managed to suppress it at the last second. He had promised not to be surprised or flustered or refuse her.

"Keh-keh! This is quite the comfortable resting place, is it not? If you were to plead and beg it of me in tears, I might consider hiring you as my personal pillow."

"L-listen, you…" he started.

"Oh-ho? Does the loser intend to disobey me?"

"Ngh…" Shido furrowed his brow, frustrated, and Kaguya guffawed in high spirits.

"Kah-kah! Such pleasure! A delight! Now shall I have you additionally stroke my hair?"

"…As you wish." He sighed in resignation, patting her head and running his fingers through her hair.

She squirmed, and her cheeks slackened as if it tickled.

"Gaah!" She flipped around so that she was facedown, wound her arms around Shido, and squeezed.

"He—" he gasped.

"I believe I said you cannot be flustered."

"Ungh…"

She was right. While Shido was quietly confused inside his own head, Kaguya stayed in this position, unmoving, for some time.

"K-Kaguya?" Shido said, timidly.

"…! Ngh. Wah…!" She began to sob softly.

"Ka…guya?"

"…! Ngh. Ungh, ungh…! Yuzuru… Yuzuru…!"

"Kaguya, are you—?" Shido said.

Kaguya sniffled and snorted before speaking in a shaky voice. "You didn't find Yuzuru. I know that much at least. Don't treat me like an idiot."

"Th-that's—"

But she kept going.

"It would be better if I didn't know. Of that, I'm certain. So I trust you. It was you who gave me and Yuzuru three options that time."

"Kaguya..."

"So...please... Yuzuru... Get Yuzuru—"

"..."

Shido gritted his teeth and put a gentle hand on her head.

Ten minutes later.

As she had announced at the start of this little adventure, Kaguya stopped crying exactly when the allotted time was up. By the time she stepped out from the shadow of the vending machines, she had completely reverted to her usual self.

She had surprising self-control. Shido stroked her hair and said, "good girl," and Kaguya replied, cheeks reddening, "Shut up."

When they were done bowling and Shido had delivered Kaguya to her apartment building, a message came in from *Fraxinus* as if they had been waiting for that moment.

...Mm, nice work, Shin."

"Thanks. Anyway, Reine," Shido said, as if to encourage her to keep her going, and Reine continued.

"...I know you just finished, but we are up against the wall here. Sorry. I'll need you to get onto your next date."

"I know. I'm definitely going to find Natsumi. And then I'll bring Yuzuru back to Kaguya." Shido clenched his hands, with new resolve.

It wasn't that he had been slacking off up to that point. But it was a fact that he did feel more determined after his date with Kaguya. The Yamai sisters needed to be together. He couldn't let anyone keep them apart, no matter who they may be.

"...Good. Head out to the next location. A coffee shop in front of the east exit at Tengu Station. We've invited the target on a date in your name, like always. She should be there in about half an hour."

"Right. Who's next?"

"...*Oh, your classmate, Ai Yamabuki.*"

Shido twitched.

Ai Yamabuki. One of the trio of girls in Shido's class. Now that Reine mentioned it, they were also suspects. But the one who was on friendly terms with them was Tohka, not Shido. He'd never really spoken with any of them one-on-one.

On top of that, it seemed that Natsumi had played all kinds of tricks on them while pretending to be Shido, so they were very much on guard against him. They were going to be troublesome, in a different way from Tonomachi.

"This is an awkward question," he said. "But how did you invite her?"

"...*Hmm? Oh, unlike with Tohka, Yoshino, and the others, I couldn't say I was asking on your behalf. So I put a note in her shoe cubby at school today.*"

"A-a note? What kind of note?"

"...'*Ai Yamabuki. I need to talk to you alone. I'll be waiting at the café by the station after school at six o'clock. Shido Itsuka,*'" Reine recited, dispassionately.

"Whoaaa." Shido pressed a hand to his forehead and groaned.

A letter like that practically begged to be misinterpreted. Actually, given that this was a date in name at least, he couldn't say that it would be a total misinterpretation.

"...*Is something the matter?*"

"No. It's nothing at all." Shido shook his head to get himself back on track.

Right. He didn't have the luxury of shrinking at something like this. What he needed to do now was investigate the remaining suspects as quickly as possible and find Natsumi. He clenched his jaw and headed toward the station.

However.

The relationship between Shido and Ai. The commotion Natsumi-as-Shido had caused. The letter of invitation sent at a time like this in Shido's name. And a girl's nature.

This all added up to...

"I knew it."

Thirty minutes later at the café by the station.

Shido felt sweat bead on his face as he watched the scene unfold just as he'd expected it to.

"What do you mean, 'I knew it'?!"

"You got a problem here?"

"What, jerk?"

In the seats across from him, in order from right to left were Ai, Mai, and Mii. He couldn't believe this had turned out just as he'd expected.

He'd had a bad feeling on the way over. Any normal girl would obviously have been on guard if she got an invitation from Shido in a letter like that in this situation. She wouldn't even dream of being so naive that she came to meet him by herself. Maybe he was just fortunate that she hadn't stood him up.

"...*Hmm. Three suspects all together then? Well, the difficulty level's a bit high, but you'll just have to investigate all three of them at once.*"

"Roger that," Shido said in a quiet voice, and turned back to the trio across from him.

At any rate, he felt like they softened up somewhat since they had ordered their favorite cake sets at his expense. But even so, the fact that they were out of sorts remained unchanged. Shido racked his brain for something to talk about.

But before he could start a conversation, the trio spoke, impatiently.

"So what exactly do you want? Sending a letter like that."

"Is that it? A love letter? What, Itsuka, you gunning for Ai?"

"Now that I'm thinking about it, you know, me and Mai only got our skirts flipped up that time, but you went and blew in Ai's ear and all."

"N-no, it's not like that." He felt like this conversation was starting to go in a weird direction.

But the trio weren't really listening to his protestations.

"Huh? For real? You and me? Uh. Uhhh. No, I mean, I appreciate it, but I'm, you know…"

"That's right. Ai's got her heart set on Kishiwada! There's no room for you to get between them!"

"Yes, exactly! Ai is in an absolutely one-sided love with the completely unthreatening, glasses-wearing Kishiwada who magnificently lets slide any invitations to hang out!"

"Hey! Both of you! You don't have to tell him that!" Ai shouted, her face beet-red. Although, well, it wasn't like Shido was going to tell anyone any of this.

"A-anyway! I don't know what you're up to, but you've got some nerve sending a letter to another girl when you've got Tohka!"

"Yeah! What, you're not satisfied with being loved by a super beautiful girl like Tohka?! You looking to be a polygamist?!"

"Oh! That reminds me. You were also eyeing Tobiichi, too, huh, Itsuka? Wait. Are you like maybe doing everyday debauchery? Whoa! Disgusting!"

The trio shrieked and scooted their chairs back, before continuing their conversation in whispers, ignoring Shido.

"That reminds me. The transfer student—was her name Tokisaki? He was flirting with her, too."

"Oh! He was, you're right! He really has *no* boundaries!"

"And, also, you know, wasn't there that mysterious little girl who brought Itsuka his lunch one time?"

"Yaah! There was! A guy who's come out as having a Lolita complex, Oedipus complex, *and* a sister complex really is different from the rest of us."

"Huh? Who's even heard of someone with so many?"

"Yeah, uh-huh. I heard that. And then also, you know. I'm pretty sure it was Itsuka? That guy who was dragged around the park by that girl from SM High with dog ears and a tail and a collar."

"For real? *I* heard he pulled down a girl's skirt."

"Eeek! I can't even believe this! How can Tohka like this guy?!"

"Oh! And also I heard from this girl in the class next door, okay…"

"H-hey…" Shido protested, weakly, but it didn't look like the trio would be done anytime soon.

"I'm exhausted."

That evening, having finished all of his dates, Shido flopped down on the sofa in his living room.

The long conversation with Ai-Mai-Mii had gone on and on and on, and when he was finally released, it was already pitch-black outside. Although he had dug into each of them somehow during the conversation, at this point, his mind and body were abnormally exhausted.

After returning home, Shido ate the supper that Kotori had prepared (it was mostly food from the supermarket deli, but Shido nearly wept with joy at the mere fact that supper was ready when he got home and at Kotori's kindness in preparing it), and took a long soak in the bath, but the exhaustion still lingered in his bones.

"Honestly, pathetic…is what I won't say, thoughtfully. Just today."

Kotori had no sooner come walking slowly out of the kitchen than something cold abruptly touched his cheek.

He was momentarily surprised, but then quickly realized that it was a can of soda that had been chilled in the fridge.

"Oh, thanks," he said.

"Uh-huh," Kotori replied, sitting down on the sofa. And then she opened the can of juice she had in her hand and gulped it down.

Shido sat up and followed suit, opening the can and letting the carbonated drink pour down his throat. The cool, invigorating liquid spread through his body.

"So? How'd the investigations go yesterday and today?" Kotori asked, turning her gaze on him.

"Mm, right." Shido dipped his head forward. "I maybe have questions about a couple of them. But I can't say anything until I check everyone out."

"Hmmm. Yeah?" she replied, surprisingly agreeable. She was going over all the conversations between Shido and the suspects, though, so she might have also gotten the same sense of something being off as Shido.

"Anyway, the investigations into everyone in the photos will end tomorrow," she said. "Go to bed early and be as fresh as you can."

"Yeah. I think I'll do just that. But…" Shido glanced at the clock on the wall. "If I go to bed now, I don't think I'll be able to get to sleep for a bit yet."

"I guess not." Kotori shrugged in agreement.

The reason was extremely simple.

The hands on the clock in the Itsuka living room were about to slide over to midnight. The time when the Angel Haniel appeared to devour Yuzuru.

Normally, they would want to have guards at the houses of everyone in the photographs, but it was obvious that this would be completely pointless when they were up against an Angel. And he couldn't say that taking her would-be hostage and putting Natsumi in a bad mood was a particularly good strategy, either.

Most likely, someone else would disappear that day.

"…"

Shido was silent as he recalled the video he'd seen on *Fraxinus* and the warmth of Kaguya's tears soaking into his knees. The helplessness. He was determined not to let Natsumi keep doing whatever she wanted like this, but he was unable to stop Haniel from swallowing up someone else. He gritted his teeth at the frustration and impatience filling his heart.

Then.

When the long and short hands of the clock clicked over to twelve, a space in the center of the Itsuka living room twisted up, and the broom-shaped Angel appeared from within the distortion.

"Wha…?!" Shido gasped and his whole body tensed. Why would the Angel be here?

But he soon hit upon a possibility. Kotori—one of the suspects—was here, wasn't she?

"Kotori!" Shido cried out, tossed his drink aside, threw his hands out, and stood in front of Haniel to protect Kotori as the tip of Haniel opened slowly to reveal its mirrored interior.

"Shido?! You can't! Get out of the way!"

But Haniel didn't try to suck Kotori in.

Instead…

"Heh-heh!"

He heard laughter from the Angel. Thinking this strange, he looked and saw Natsumi's face in the mirrored interior.

"Natsumi?!"

"Heeere. Been a while, hmm, Shido?" Natsumi said, in a familiar manner, and waved, the corners of her mouth turning up. *"It's the end of day two of the game. I hope you're having fun?"*

Shido gritted his teeth. "What exactly are you up to?"

"What am I up to?"

"What did you do with Yuzuru?" he asked, and Natsumi giggled and shrugged.

"That. Is a Se. Cret. If you actually guess who I am, I'll give her back. But if you can't figure out which one is me by the end, well, her existence will belong to me."

"Her 'existence'…?" Shido asked, frowning.

"Yes." Natsumi nodded, leisurely. *"If I win this game, then the disappeared suspects won't come back. Instead, I'll have a bit of fun in that world with their faces, voices, figures—everything."*

"…!"

Shido swallowed hard.

A fake undetectably close to the real person strutting around a world without that person in it. Natsumi could easily impersonate the real Yuzuru and whoever else she disappeared.

"Not a chance. I won't let you do that!" Shido said, his gaze growing sharper.

Natsumi laughed, merrily. *"Then what you have to do is simple. Go on and guess who I am. Who do you think it is? As for a time limit, hmm, right. A minute should be plenty."*

Shido and Kotori looked at each other with a gasp.

"Guess?! Now?!"

"Does seem that way," Kotori said, glaring at Natsumi.

Natsumi shrugged and laughed. *"Hee hee! I mean, Shido's so annoying! He didn't pick anyone in the end on the first day. So I have to guide him a little, is what I figured."*

"Hmph. You've got some nerve." Kotori snorted. But as if grasping that this was not the time for that sort of thing, she quickly turned her gaze on Shido. "How about it? You said you had your doubts about someone just a minute ago."

"Yeah. That's true, but I still don't have—"

"If you don't say anything, today will end with another person disappearing. Pick a name. You've got nothing to lose," Kotori urged him.

Shido turned this over in his mind and then nodded. "Right."

He looked at Natsumi in Haniel's mirror.

"Natsumi. The person you turned into is...Yoshino."

"Yoshino?" Kotori parroted.

"Yeah." Shido continued, his eyes still on Natsumi. "Out of those I checked out yesterday and today, the person who felt the most off to me was Yoshino."

"I'll just ask then. Why?"

"She was the one acting the least like herself."

That said, however, he had no definitive proof. She had only felt off compared with everyone else. He felt bad for treating her like a criminal on that basis alone. But it was also true that there was no one else he found suspicious at the present moment.

"Hmm." was all Natsumi said after hearing Shido's response, and then she snapped her fingers.

The end of Haniel closed and the broom had no sooner returned to its original shape than it was melting into the air.

"She disappeared?! What does this mean? Was your answer right? Did you get it wrong?" Kotori frowned, dubiously.

But there was no one who could answer her.

＊　　　＊　　　＊

And then that night.

Two girls disappeared from their beds.

◇

The next day, October 24.

In contrast with the fine weather, Shido's mood was at rock-bottom.

But that was only natural. Because he had gotten a notification from Ratatoskr that Haniel had taken two girls the previous night—Yoshino and Ai.

"Yoshino... Yamabuki... Because of me," Shido groaned to himself.

"...You're wrong," Reine said through the earpiece in his right ear. *"You did good with the limited information you had. It's not your fault."*

"But...didn't Yoshino disappear because...I named her?"

When Ratatoskr told them that two girls had disappeared, one more than the previous night, this was the first hypothesis Shido and Kotori landed on. They conjectured that one person would disappear each night, with another person also vanishing if Shido guessed wrong.

"...There's a strong possibility that's the case. But Shin, it's—"

"It's okay. I know. It's not the same thing. It's not like Natsumi will raise her hand and identify herself if I don't pick someone. And if I keep pulling this long face, it'll be an insult to the busy idol who's sharing her precious time with me," Shido said, his face tense as he forced a grin.

His first date that day was with the super popular idol, Miku Izayoi.

"...Mm. Right. Sorry, Shin."

"Why are you apologizing, Reine?"

"...I thought I understood your strength and growth, but I went and let my imagination get the best of me again." Reine laughed, self-deprecatingly.

Shido was embarrassed for some reason at this unusual reaction from Reine and scratched his cheek as he looked around the area. "Y-you know…there are a lot of unusual-looking people here."

Shido was waiting for Miku in the central plaza of Ocean Park, the theme park where he'd once gone on a date with Kotori. But for some reason, there were a strangely remarkable number of guests wearing curious outfits. And there hadn't been the last time he was here.

On top of that, they weren't simply showing off quirky fashions. They were all dressed as anime or manga characters he'd seen before. Yes. In slang terms, this was the so-called "costume play."

"…*Aah, that's—*"

"Daaaarliiiiiiing!"

He heard a familiar voice drown out Reine's, coming from the plaza entrance. Miku.

Shido turned his face that way, raised his hand. "Hey—Huh?"

When he saw the girl running toward him, his jaw dropped.

He had to assume that the girl in the frilly costume with keynotes of white and purple was Miku. The reason he couldn't say for sure was simple. She was wearing a mask that covered her eyes. She looked almost like she was heading to a masked ball.

"Miku…right? What's with the outfit?" Shido asked, and she sniffed haughtily before taking on an adorable pose.

"What do you thiiiink? It looks good on me, right? I'm the fourth of the *Valkyrie Misty* warrior maidens, Kanon Tsukishima. It's the rare masked version from when she appears to save the Misties in episode siiiix!"

"Huh? Oh. Huh?" Shido furrowed his brow, dubiously.

"Honestly!" Miku puffed out her cheeks, sulkily. "You don't know *Valkyrie Misty*? It's an anime for girls that airs on Friday mornings."

Shido's brow relaxed at this. "Oh! Now that you mention it, I feel like Yoshino used to watch that."

"What? Yoshino likes *Misty*, toooo? Hee-hee-hee! That's a useful thing to know. I'll have to inviiiiite her next time!" Miku said happily before breaking into a smile.

Shido hedged and then pointed at her outfit. "So then why are you dressed as Kanon?"

"Hmm? Didn't Reine teeeell you? They're having a Halloween event at Ocean Park this week. You're allowed to wear costuuuumes!"

"Huh? Really?" Shido's eyes grew wide. But this made sense. That would be the reason why he'd seen so many cosplayers walking around. "Oh, okay. Is that it? Still, I didn't know you liked cosplay, Miku."

"Well, there is that. But, you know, I'm famous, soooo."

"Oh. Right." He was convinced. Not only were people wearing masks, some were even dressed up as robots. It was true that in a place like this, it wasn't the least bit strange for Miku to hide her face.

"Well, I don't particularly miiind if anyone realizes it's me," she told him. "But you seemed worried about it, darling. And wouldn't it be awful if someone were to interrupt our precious daaaate?"

"Ha-ha!" Shido gave her a pained smile. "Oh, well, yeah, thanks for being so thoughtful."

Miku clapped her hands like she'd just remembered something. "I have a men's costuuuume for you in my locker in the changing room. The cloak and mask of Lord Sieg, the mysterious hero who helps the Misties when they're in a tight spot! I'll go get it, so you can get changed, too!"

"Huh?" He frowned. "N-no, I'm good, actually."

"Then you could use my backup costume, the second warrior maiden, Mei Narusaki—"

"Lord Sieg sounds cool! I'd love to wear that one!" Shido cried out in a shrill voice. He couldn't stand the idea of being put into all those ruffles.

Miku beamed at him, delighted.

"Eeek!" Miku shrieked and jumped around when he came out of the locker room after he'd changed. "Amaaaazing! It looks so good on you! You look so cooool, darling!"

"I-I do?" Shido said awkwardly.

He was wearing a jet-black, floor-length coat, a mask that hid his face, and a long wig. About the only part of him that was still touching the outside air were his ears.

"Doesn't everyone look the same in this, though? I mean, as long as you're basically the same size?"

"Nooooo! That's not true! The aura you radiate is diiiiifferent!"

"Aura…huh?" He raised a skeptical eyebrow.

"Yes!" Miku insisted. "The truth is, even though Lord Sieg dresses like this, his true identity is the sixth warrior maiden Emily Kano."

"Hey! Hold on a second. You never told me that."

"Ha-ha-ha! Oh, didn't I?" Miku stuck out her tongue adorably.

The way she looked, he couldn't be angry with her.

Well, at least she hadn't made him wear a skirt.

More importantly, now they could finally start their date. From behind the mask that covered his face, Shido said, "Woh-kay. So, Miku. We can't stand in front of the changing rooms forever. How about we get moving? It is a date, after all. Let's talk."

"Okay! With pleasure!" Miku said, happily, and snaked her arm through his. She snuggled in close and they began to walk.

Maybe it's good that we're in masks and costumes, Shido thought, his cheeks likely reddening, and began to ask his questions.

"Hey, Miku? You remember the first time we met? When you were singing all by yourself at Tengu Arena?"

"Yes, of course I do!" She nodded, beaming.

Shido smiled behind his mask and continued. "You've been like this since we first met, I guess. I was surprised when you up and hugged me like that."

"Hmm?" Miku's eyes grew round in surprise. "Did that happen? I'm pretty sure back then, I hated boys more than anything in this world, though."

"So that doesn't trip you up?" he murmured.

"Did you say something, darliiiing?"

"No, it's nothing. Right, I must be remembering wrong," Shido said, and looked at Miku to ask his next question.

"Umm. Excuse me?"

Two girls dressed like Miku appeared before them.

"You're Kanon and Lord Sieg, right?" one of them said, timidly. "If you don't mind, could we take your picture?"

"Uh. Umm." Shido scratched his head, unsure. He was one thing, but Miku was an idol. Although she had her face hidden with her mask, maybe it was better if they avoided this kind of—

But Miku assented to their request readily, undermining Shido's thinking. "We don't mind at aaaall. Just be sure to make it a good picture!"

"Th-thank you so much! Okay then." One of the girls said and held up her camera.

Shido hurriedly whispered in Miku's ear. "Hey, are you sure? I mean, a photo?"

"It's fiiiiine. My face is hidden, after all. Come on now, darling. Pose, pose," Miku replied, in high spirits, and began to give Shido detailed instructions. He wrapped an arm around Miku's waist and was forced into an extremely unstable pose, like the big finish for a couple in a pair skating performance.

"H-hey, I feel like we're going to fall over here," he whispered.

"Don't woooorry. Now, please go ahead and take the picture!" Miku said with a smile, and the girl snapped several pictures in succession.

"Oh! Do you mind if I get this angle, too?! Please look this way!"

"Sure, go ahead," Miku responded to the girl's request and leaned back. And caused a sudden load to be imposed on Shido's arm so that he lost his already precarious balance completely.

"Whoa!"

"Eeek!"

He fell to the ground as if pushed over by Miku.

"S-sorry!" he cried. "Are you okay?!"

"Mmm. Oh, darling! You're. So. Bold! ♥" Miku flushed and poked Shido's masked nose. It seemed that she was uninjured.

"Looks like you're fine, huh?" he said, almost rolling his eyes, as he stood up and then helped Miku to her feet.

Then he realized something was off.

The girls who had been taking their picture were frozen in place, jaws dropped, eyes wide.

"Miku-tan…?" one of them breathed.

"No way. Are you real?"

"…?!"

Shido gasped and looked at Miku. Right. Why had Shido known that her cheeks were turning red a second ago?

The reason was simple. When she fell over, the mask hiding her face had come off.

"Oh dear," Miku said, remarkably calm, as the girls' surprise radiated outward to the surrounding cosplayers.

"Huh? Miku? You mean, *the* Miku?"

"Like Miku Izayoi cosplay? Huh? Wait, the *real* Miku?"

"Whoa! For real? I'm a huge fan."

"And like, who is that with her? A boy? A girl?"

The area immediately exploded into chatter.

"Ngh! We're getting out of here, Miku!" Shido grimaced behind his mask, grabbed Miku's hand, and started to run.

But Miku tugged on his hand to stop him.

"Wh-what's wrong?" he asked. "If we stay here, you'll be swarmed."

"Mmm. I think I twisted my ankle a little."

"Huh? But a second ago, you were—" Shido started, and Miku pressed her index finger to the mouth area of his mask.

"All. Twisted. Uuuup. So please carry me."

"H-huh?!" Shido's eyes flew open at this sudden request. "Y-you, what…"

"Cooome on," she pleaded. "If you don't hurry, people will crowd around and then we won't be able to get away, you know?"

"Ngh!" He gritted his teeth, slid his arms around her shoulders and legs, and put his back into it. In slang terms, what is known as the so-called "princess carry." And then he raced out of the venue.

"Eeek! Darling, you're so daaaashing!" Miku yelped with delight and wrapped her arms around his neck.

"I told you not to call me 'darling' where other people can hear!" Shido half-shouted as he ran through the theme park overrun with cosplayers.

In the end, it took a fair bit of time and effort carrying Miku to shake the cosplayers.

Although it was a weekday, there were people all over Ocean Park who wanted to show off their own transformations. There was a wall of people ahead of them, and Shido and Miku had to go around somehow.

They made it to the washrooms and succeeded in escaping that tight spot by putting Miku into Shido's costume. But by that time, Shido was utterly exhausted.

He didn't have the option of a leisurely rest, however.

He finished his date with Miku. The time was five o'clock. He changed into his uniform and headed to the school, where classes were already over. He was going to meet his next target—Tama.

"*...As with the others, we've already made contact with Ms. Okamine. She should be waiting for you in the counseling office.*"

"Roger. I'll go there now," Shido replied, briefly, and walked through the deserted school.

On his way, a small worry abruptly popped up in his head.

"That reminds me. What reason did you give her for asking her to meet?" he timidly asked his earpiece.

Yes. Just like Ai-Mai-Mii, Tama was someone Shido had never asked out before. He was concerned about exactly what kind of message Reine had sent.

"*...Oh. I basically told her you wanted to talk about your options after graduation.*"

"Makes sense. That's pretty natural." He let out a sigh of relief and headed for the designated location.

Before too long, he had arrived at the counseling office. He knocked on the door and soon heard Tama's cute voice from inside. "Come in!"

"Excuse me." He opened the door and went in. He saw Tama sitting on the sofa with what appeared to be student worksheets spread out on the table in front of her. It seemed that she had been grading papers while she waited for him.

"Oh! Itsuka. I haven't seen you in a while," Tama said, smiling, as she pulled the worksheets together into a pile and pushed the graduation-related books on the edge of the table to the side.

Shido did feel something slightly off at her greeting, but it was nothing serious. He had been absent from school that day and the day before in order to search for Natsumi.

"Well, please sit down."

"Thanks." He sat on the sofa opposite her.

"Let's see." With a meek look on her face, Tama pushed the bridge of her glasses up. "I heard from Ms. Murasame that you wanted to talk about your options after graduation."

"Yes." Shido nodded. "Would you mind discussing them a bit?"

"I don't mind at all." Tama got a slightly complicated look on her face. "But why me and not the guidance counselor?"

"Huh? Oh, umm," Shido stammered.

Now that she mentioned it, that was true. There was a guidance counselor at the high school for exactly this sort of thing. If he had questions about anything, normally that was who he would talk to. But if he reacted honestly, there was a chance that she might hand him off to the guidance counselor.

He clenched his fists and spoke. "Oh, it's just, well, it has to be you, Ms. Okamine!"

"What?!" For some reason, Tama's face was flush with surprise. She looked like her heart had leaped in her chest, but in a happy way. "The *guidance* counselor…has to be me?"

"Yes. There's no meaning in it without you," Shido said forcefully, and Tama suddenly appeared overexcited.

"Uh! Uh? S-so then, you mean, ma—"

"Huh?"

"N-no! It's nothing!" Tama hurriedly shook her head.

Bewildered, Shido cocked his head to the side.

At any rate, it was just the two of them now. He should check sooner rather than later whether or not this was the real Tama. Shido made this decision and sent his mind racing—he decided he would try asking about when she had become Shido's homeroom teacher, to start.

"Umm, Ms. Okamine. I just wanted to check something. Do you remember what happened in April?"

"April... Oh!" Her eyes flew open, and she nodded so vigorously that he worried her head might fall off. "I do remember! I remember! Have you finally...made up your mind, Itsuka?"

"Uh?" Shido stared vacantly at this unexpected reaction.

Tama pulled several books out of her bag and spread them out on the table in front of Shido. "I grabbed a bunch of books about options for your future after graduation. Please let me know if you have aspirations toward anything in them!"

"Oh, uh, I..." Shido tried to go back to his question, but then he took a closer look at the books that Tama had set out about his "options."

The first book had a beautiful bride on the cover. Did she mean some bridal-related work then?

The second book. What looked to be a married couple with an adorable baby graced the cover. So this was...a guide to an early childhood education program...probably.

And the third book. Although it wasn't so much a book as it was a document. The words *marriage license application* shone at the top, and the name of the bride had already been penned in, complete with official seal.

"Wha...?!" Once he saw this, Shido finally realized that Tama had gotten the absolute wrong idea. The most ridiculous one possible.

Now that he was thinking about it, though, at the instruction of Ratatoskr, Shido had been forced in April to tell Tama he liked her (he had essentially proposed).

"Uh. Umm, Ms. Okamine?" he said.

"Itsuka, I'm so happy! I knew you'd come around. It was so sudden then, so maybe you lost your nerve, but I knew you'd come back to me once things settled down! Aah! All the work I put into getting things ready was worth it! Hey, Itsuka? When should we meet each other's parents? Oh! Before that, here. How about we fill this out? Hmm? Personal seal? That's okay, I got that ready for you, too. Please don't worry. We won't bring it into city hall until you're actually eighteen!"

Eyes shining brightly, Tama grabbed the sleeve of his blazer.

Shido squeaked and sprang to his feet.

"I-I'm sorry I gave you the wrong ideaaaaaa!" he cried and left the room.

In the counseling office, Tama was still laying out their future family plans, ecstatically.

7:00 PM. Shido was walking down the dark roads of town for his date with the next target.

The twelfth suspect. With this date, the investigation into the people in the photos would be complete.

"…"

As he walked along silently, he put a hand to his chin and considered the situation. The remaining suspects were Tohka, Tonomachi, Kotori, Kaguya, Mai, Mii, Miku, Tama, and then this twelfth person for a total of nine.

That day, he had gone on dates with Miku and Tama. Miku remembered what happened with they first met, and although he hadn't been able to talk much with Tama, it seemed that she did remember his outpouring of love in April. He had a hard time believing that either of them was Natsumi.

Which meant that the last person he was meeting now was Natsumi…didn't it? Or did it mean that Natsumi had the power to read a person's memories?

If that were the case, then his investigation was right back at square one. And not only would he have to rethink how to find Natsumi, but Haniel would take someone else at the end of the day.

He couldn't put his finger on it, though. Since he'd started this investigation three days earlier, he'd had this tiny feeling smoldering in his head like something was off somehow.

A whodunnit game with no clues. Each day, one person disappeared, and if he guessed the wrong person to be the culprit, that person also disappeared. And he had to find Natsumi among the suspects before they *all* were taken away.

Was this really the way the game was supposed to be played?

Something about all this was bugging him. But he didn't know what that something was. Feeling a bit sick, Shido ran his hands through his hair.

"...*Shin, you're almost there.*"

"... Ah..." He jerked his head up at the sound of Reine's voice. He'd walked quite a ways while lost in thought. It was amazing he hadn't walked into anything.

He took a deep breath, admonishing himself, and from up ahead—from the destination he was walking toward, he heard a familiar voice.

"Shido."

"Hey, Origami." Shido waved a hand in response and headed toward the final suspect—Origami Tobiichi. "Sorry. Were you waiting long?"

Origami shook her head slightly. "I just got here."

"...*We were keeping watch. She's been waiting for an hour,*" Reine said, as if to supplement her answer.

Shido smiled, lifelessly.

"...? What's wrong?"

"O-oh," he said. "You know. I was just thinking it's been ages since I went out with you."

"Oh." Origami said and nodded before continuing, the look on her face completely unchanged. "I'm happy, too."

"Y-yeah..."

She looked the same as always, but having known her for a long time now, Shido had come to understand the subtle changes in Origami's mood. His heart hurt a little at his extremely insincere action, a date for the sake of his investigation.

"So what are we seeing?" She looked up at the building she'd been waiting in front of. It was adorned with several enormous movie billboards.

Yes. His date with Origami was at a movie theater.

"Mm. Right," he said. "I don't know yet."

"You haven't decided?" Origami's eyebrow arched up.

Crap. He held his breath. It was too unnatural that he had asked her out but hadn't decided on what they would see. Or too indecisive.

"Oh, sorry, that's not what I mean. Uh. Right." Shido panicked. "Let's see this one! I've watched the trailers."

Origami continued quietly. "Does this mean that you didn't ask me out because there was a movie you wanted to see, but because you wanted to go out with me?"

"Huh? Oh. Right...I guess it does," he replied, vaguely.

"..."

Origami jumped up on the spot, just once, the expression on her face unchanged. And then she whirled around and marched into the movie theater.

"H-hey, Origami?"

"Come." She led Shido to the ticket counter, stood in front of an open clerk, and held up two fingers. "Two *lovers'* tickets to *Black Fantasy* starting at seven-thirty."

"What?" The eyes of the ticket clerk grew round in surprise. "Er. Umm. So that would be two adult tickets then?"

"That would be fine," Origami said, smoothly.

"O-okay. Then your total is 3,600 yen."

Origami took the tickets and handed one to Shido. "Here."

"Uh. Umm... Thanks. Oh! But I asked you out. I'll pay." Shido moved to grab his wallet, and Origami stopped him.

"Later's fine," she said.

"Huh?" His eyes widened in surprise, as Origami walked off toward the counter where they sold drinks and snacks.

Unable to get what she was up to, he stood there stunned and then heard Reine's voice in his right ear.

"*...I see. So she's not planning to let you go home even after the movie ends.*"

"..."

Shido felt a strange chill run up his spine.

"H-hey, Origami? You remember that thing in June?"

Shido said to Origami in the seat next to him to try and dig deeper, right before the start of the movie, once the trailers began playing.

"In June?" she asked.

"Yeah. You know. We went on a date then once, too, right?"

"Of course I remember."

Really? What did we do again?" he said, and Origami nodded, perfunctorily.

"Eleven hundred hours. Meeting in front of fountain in the plaza at Tengu station. Eleven-ten. Restaurant to eat lunch. Eleven-eleven. Shido goes to the washroom. Twelve hundred hours. Movie theater. Twelve-ten. Shido washroom again. Thinking that you were having stomach trouble, purchase of medication in pharmacy at fourteen-twenty. Fifteen hundred hours—"

"H-hang on a sec." As Origami rattled off the events of their date, he tried to slow her down for a second. "How can you remember it in such detail?"

Origami nodded, sharply, before digging into the bag she was carrying. She pulled what looked like a book out from inside.

"What's that?" he asked.

"Journal," she said, briefly, and handed the book to Shido, opening it as if to say, "read it."

He looked at the text and saw that she had indeed noted the details of the situation in one-minute increments.

"W-wow."

With a pained smile, he flipped through the journal. The entries for the day he told her he liked her and the day when he first visited her house were particularly long, about five times the length of an average entry.

"Ungh." A bead of sweat trickled down his cheek when he saw that entry. It said that when she inspected her room after Shido left, the rabbit puppet she'd found a few days earlier was gone. That would have been Yoshinon. There was even an illustration. It was definitely Yoshinon.

Although it had been for Yoshino's sake, he had basically been stealing, and his heart hurt. But he felt a little better somehow at seeing "the glorious day Shido took something of mine with him" inscribed below this entry.

"With something like this, this Origami has to be the real thing, huh?" he murmured.

"...*We still don't know. The one who made the journal is the real Origami Tobiichi, but just the fact that she has it now doesn't mean that she's necessarily the real Origami.*"

"Well...I guess you're right." Shido clapped the journal shut and gave it back to Origami.

The screen abruptly went dark, and solemn music began to play. It seemed that the main attraction was beginning.

Shido felt something soft touch the back of his hand. Origami had placed her own hand on top of his.

"Ha-ha..." He laughed, weakly, but didn't try to brush it off. In fact, holding his hand during a movie was such an extremely cute thing for Origami to do that he actually found it sweet.

However. Shido's thinking was too naive.

"..."

Origami's hand squirmed along bit by bit as the movie progressed.

The hand that had at first simply rested on his now stroked the back of it. And then it traced out each of his fingers affectionately before at last tangling finger with finger in an extremely erotic manner.

"Eee?!"

She was only touching up to the base of his right wrist, but Shido felt electric currents racing through his entire body. A sensation that mixed ticklishness with pleasure pushed over him in waves and made his vision flicker.

"Shido…"

He heard a voice whisper in his ear. He tried desperately not to look in that direction. "Wh-wh-wh-wh-wh-what is it?"

"I want you to touch me, too."

"T-touch," he said, in a shaky voice.

Origami pulled down the neck of her shirt. "I'm not wearing anything today."

"…?!"

Shido gasped. His brain started to spin full throttle and threatened to short-circuit. His face turned so red, he was sure smoke was shooting out of his ears.

He took a deep breath to try and calm himself down, and then fumbled around to find the iced tea he'd bought earlier and get the straw in his mouth to wet his bone-dry throat.

But no matter how he sucked, he did not taste chilled tea in his mouth.

Thinking this strange, he took a look at his hand and quickly understood the reason. The straw in his cup of iced tea was not the one in his mouth.

So then what exactly was it…

He looked and saw that the end of the straw was in the mouth of Origami leaning forward toward him.

Without a word, Origami sucked on the straw.

"Whoa?!" Shido cried out and leaped up from his seat. The prickly stares of the audience members around him stabbed into him.

"What's wrong?" Origami asked.

"Wh-what's wrong?! You…"

"…*This is*…"

"*She's real, all right.*"

"*No doubt about it*…"

In Shido's right ear, the crew of *Fraxinus* unanimously recognized this as the true Origami.

◇

In the end, it wasn't until 11:00 PM that Shido was released by Origami.

Staggering down the dark road, he made it back to his own home.

"Today was…extra difficult," he muttered to himself, stretching. The bones in his shoulders cracked.

After the movie, they had gone to a nearby café and chatted for a while. And as he'd already discovered, Origami memorized every detail of the time she spent with him. With incredible accuracy, like she was replaying a recorded movie. There was also the matter of her assertiveness. It really did look like Origami was not Natsumi.

But that meant he was back to square one. He'd gone on dates with all of the suspects, but there was no clear culprit.

"Shido!" Tohka called out to him when he was opening the gate to the Itsuka house, deep in thought. She was in her pajamas at the entrance of the apartment building next door.

"Tohka?" he said. "What are you doing out here at this hour?"

"I could ask you the same thing. Where exactly were you out so late?" she said, walking toward him. She didn't sound angry, just genuinely curious.

"Oh. Sorry, I was just out," he replied, evasively.

"Mm…" Tohka puffed up her cheeks, unhappily. "You've been so busy the past couple of days. You haven't come to school, and you haven't been making me lunch or supper, either."

"S-sorry. Once I finish up with some stuff, I'll cook for you again. Okay?" He clapped his hands together and bowed.

She hurriedly shook her head. "No, that's fine. That's not what's bothering me. Hmm? Oh! You're right that I want to eat your cooking though, so you're not wrong, I guess?"

She craned her neck from side to side, as if wrestling with this thought. But then she lifted her face again and grabbed Shido's hand.

"Anyway! You've got a lot to deal with, right? Don't worry about me. I've decided not to fight with Origami Tobiichi, and I'm eating alright. So you do what you have to do, Shido."

"Tohka…," he said.

She blushed. "But when you're never around, it's, like… I get lonely.

Tell me if there's anything I can do. I'll come running no matter what it is if it's for you, Shido!" She gave his hand a squeeze.

The way she looked at him so openly and spoke to him so honestly made him impossibly happy, and he squeezed her hand back.

"Yeah, thanks, Tohka," he said. "With you on my side, I've basically got the strength of an army."

"Mm." She smiled with real delight. "That's all I wanted to say! So g'night, Shido! Natsuuumi!"

For a second, he jumped, but then he remembered his fib to her.

"Yeah, good night, Tohka. Natsuuumi!"

Shido waved, and Tohka flung her arm around in the air in a wave ten times more energetic than his and ran back to the apartment building. And then yawning hugely, she went inside.

She really had waited up until now just to tell him she was there for him. Tohka, the girl who always went to bed early.

He felt a mix of remorse and fondness and mild amusement well up in him, and he smiled a little. His step felt a little lighter than it had a couple minutes ago somehow.

He slipped through the gate, pulled his keys out of his pocket, and opened the door.

"You're late," his queenly little sister said, hands on hips in an intimidating pose, as if she had been waiting there for exactly this moment.

"Don't come at me like that," he replied. "I've been run ragged over here."

"I know that. I mean, I obviously understand the situation, and it's not like I'm mad or anything. It's just—" She sighed and continued, brow knit in annoyance. "It's nearly time."

The moment she said this, the space between Shido and Kotori twisted, and the broom-shaped Angel appeared.

"Ngh," Kotori groaned. "There it is."

"Haniel? It's already midnight?!" Shido scowled and gritted his teeth. It had apparently taken him a while to get home.

However, the silver lining was that Haniel hadn't appeared while Tohka was here. He took a deep breath to calm himself down and turned toward the Angel.

As he did, Haniel opened up one end to expose the mirrored interior to the outside world. And then, just like the day before, he saw Natsumi reflected there.

"Helllllloooo. It's been a whole day, Shido. Did you miss me?"

"Natsumi... You...!"

"Ooh! Scary face! Shall we have a little more fun with our game?" Natsumi said and grinned, merrily.

Shido clenched his hands so tightly his fingernails dug into his palms, so he exhaled to keep himself under control. Getting emotional here and now would solve nothing. Not only that, it was even possible that doing so would cause harm to Yuzuru and the others who had been taken by Haniel. He had to watch what he said.

"Hee hee!" Natsumi giggled *"The third day of the game's over, hmm? I hope you've investigated everyone? So answer me. Who am I?"*

"...!"

Shido swallowed hard and recalled the faces of the suspects he'd dated over the past three days. But he couldn't come up with an answer. Although he'd checked them all out, he still didn't have any clear evidence against any of them.

"Shido, you're out of time," Kotori said.

"I know," he replied, as he eliminated suspects in his head one after the other.

The last one standing was Tama.

She did appear to remember his outpouring of love in April, but it wasn't like she'd actually said it in so many words. When he went over her behavior over the last few days, it seemed like her rush to get married was the focus, and that was something that Natsumi could have found out rather easily. Thinking about it like this, Tama's over-the-top approach could have been a way of freaking Shido out to keep him from digging too deep.

Shido glared at Haniel and opened his mouth. "Natsumi, you are—"

But the face of Yoshino flitted through his mind, and he stopped. Shido had named her the day before, and because of that, Haniel had taken her.

If he was wrong about Tama, then he would have once again dragged someone else into this mess.

At best, he had doubts about Tama. It wasn't like he had any decisive proof. Not to mention that when he started to say her name, that nagging feeling that had been hanging over him like a heavy fog got even stronger and strangled his thoughts.

Something's missing. I'm making some kind of fundamental mistake.

This unfounded anxiety caused him to stop speaking.

"Shido!" Kotori cried.

"…!"

His eyes flew open. But it was too late.

Natsumi made a big X with her hands. *"Ennnh! Time's up. That's too bad. Try again tomorrow, okaaay?"*

The air shimmered once more, and Haniel vanished. The Itsuka siblings were left alone in the entryway of their house, silently rooted to the spot.

After a while, Kotori shook her head and sighed. "I don't blame you. I mean, knowing that if you get it wrong, that person will disappear, it's hard to answer without having some kind of hard evidence. But…" she continued. "Just remember that a bunch of people have already been taken, and that the game won't end unless you find Natsumi."

"Yeah… Sorry."

Kotori was right. Shido cursed his own indecisiveness and ran his hands through his hair. And then he heard Reine's voice in his right ear.

"…Shin. Can you hear me, Shin?"

"Reine…? What's up?"

"…Haniel appeared on one of the autonomous cameras monitoring the suspects."

Shido felt his heart constrict. He should have known. It was just like the previous day. After he gave his answer, Haniel took one of the suspects. He thought he had understood that. But his heart still pounded painfully now.

"…So who—" *Disappeared today?* He couldn't finish his question.

Even though it wasn't like this would change anything, he couldn't make himself utter the words. It was like his body itself was rejecting the statement.

"...*Mm-hmm. The one who disappeared today...*" Reine broke off, as if trying to decide whether or not she should tell him, and then continued,

"...*is Tohka.*"

"Huh?" Shido could practically hear his own body cracking apart.

Chapter 5
Witchcraft

One of the many Ratatoskr-owned buildings in a suburb of Tengu City.

Woodman was visiting basement level three.

"This way, Lord Woodman." A young staff member led him to the end of a long hallway and stopped in front of a cramped space, sectioned off with iron bars. Essentially, it was a jail cell.

There was a man lying on a bed inside. Middle-aged, wearing simple clothes. Several recently-acquired injuries marked his face and body.

"This is the DEM employee captured two months ago during the Arubi Island incident," the staff member said. "We know from the identification he had on his person that he is James A. Paddington, colonel in the second enforcement division, but we haven't been able to learn anything else."

"Nothing?" Woodman arched an eyebrow. "You mean he's refusing to talk?"

"I'm not certain it's that deliberate." The staff member looked troubled and banged on the iron bars. Only Paddington showed absolutely no reaction. "He's been like this since his capture. We tried questioning him with a Realizer a number of times, but it's as though his memories have been knocked right out of his head."

"I see." Woodman nodded. "That does sound like something he would do."

"'He,' sir?" The staff member cocked their head inquisitively.

"Never mind," Woodman replied. "Do you mind if I talk with him a bit?"

"Ah, you're more than welcome to, but…" The staff member stepped back with a dubious look on their face.

Woodman asked Karen to turn his wheelchair to face Paddington in the cell. "Hey there, James," he said. "Could we chat for a minute?"

"…!"

Although he had been utterly unresponsive up until that point, Paddington now sat up on the bed like a spring-loaded doll.

"Gaah?!" The staff member yelped, startled.

But Paddington paid them no attention. Instead, he staggered toward Woodman on unsteady feet and fell forward against the bars. Unfocused eyes and lips covered in drool were pressed toward Woodman.

"Ah. Ah. Aaaaah. Aaaaaaaah. Oo. Oo. Ooooo. Dddd. Ma. Ma. Man," Paddington spoke like a broken record, his voice deep in his throat, and twitched his head.

But a few seconds later, the discordant sound coming out of him stabilized into something that could be taken as a voice.

And then.

"Well, hello. Been a while, hmm, Elliot?" He spoke in a different voice. Actually, the word *spoke* might not have been correct. Paddington's face had not changed. Although he was speaking, his lips and even his tongue were not moving. It was more apt to say that another voice was coming out of a human-shaped speaker.

"Wh—Th-this…" the staff member cried out, baffled.

Well, that was no wonder. Woodman shrugged slightly before replying to Paddington—no, more accurately speaking, to the man on the other end of the line.

"Mm-hmm. Thirty years. You good, Ike?"

"As I ever was. How about you, Elliot?"

"Not so sure about myself. My eyes've gotten a fair bit worse lately."

"Well, that's not good news."

He chatted with the mysterious voice coming from the man in a zombie-like state, and the staff member watched from off to the side, disturbed.

"By the way, Elliot. I suppose you're not thinking of coming back to us? I'm sure you're aware of the fact that Princess inverted. We are this close to realizing all of our dreams. And we would be that much closer if we had your assistance. I'm sure Ellen would also be delighted to have you back."

"Unfortunately, I'm not planning on it, Ike. We hashed all of that out thirty years ago," Woodman said, and the voice sighed regretfully.

"Too bad. It seems that you still haven't recovered from the fever that ravaged you, even after thirty years' time."

Paddington's body started to slide down the iron bars.

"In that case, I'll show no mercy the next time we come face-to-face. I will use the Spirits for the sake of our goal."

"I won't let you do that," Woodman replied, firmly. "That's why Ratatoskr exists."

"Heh..."

The voice stopped. Paddington collapsed to the floor and blood gushed from his mouth.

"Wha—?!" Gobsmacked, the staff member tapped at a terminal and began communicating with the upper floors.

Woodman furrowed his brow ever so slightly. "You haven't changed, Ike. Everything's exactly as it was thirty years ago." And then without turning his head, he spoke to the woman holding the wheelchair grips. "Might be that a direct confrontation with DEM is coming in the near future. Make sure you're ready, Karen."

"It will not be a problem. I understood some years ago that my sister and I cannot come to an understanding," Karen Nora Mathers replied, no change in the tone of her voice.

At the same time, in a room in the DEM Industries UK head office, managing director Isaac Westcott sighed. And then he pushed a button and called someone in from outside.

In mere seconds, there was a knock on the door.

"Excuse me," Ellen said, as she came into the room. "Did you need something, Ike?"

"Oh. It's nothing major," Westcott said, turning his gaze toward her. "I was just thinking Murdock had a point at the board meeting earlier."

"By which you mean?"

"It's a fact that we lost a large number of Wizards in that operation," he replied. "The loss of Adeptus Two Mana Takamiya and Adeptus Three Jessica Bailey, in particular, pose a very significant problem in targeting the Spirits going forward."

"So you're suggesting replacement personnel?" Ellen asked, arching an eyebrow faintly. He was not mistaken in seeing a hint of displeasure color her expression.

He shrugged. "Naturally, as long as I have you, everything will proceed smoothly. But think of it as insurance. After all, it's true that you would have an easier time of it if you had support, yes?"

"..."

Ellen exhaled quietly before turning her eyes on Westcott once more. "Then who exactly? Where would we find a Wizard with the power befitting a DEM Adeptus number? If you're thinking of SSS's Artemisia, unfortunately—"

"No." He cut her off, the corners of his lips turning upward. "There is someone, isn't there? A surprising Wizard who managed to hurt you."

He could hear the chirping of a sparrow from outside his room.

"..."

Without a word, Shido glanced at the morning sun peeking in through his window and then turned his eyes back to the data on his computer screen and the impossible number of papers scattered around him.

These noted comprehensive information on the suspects and their reactions to Shido. Physical data like height, weight, blood type, the positions of moles; place of birth; family structure; current address and surrounding environment; and a detailed list of preferences, hobbies, and even fetishes—Ratatoskr had dug up all of this with no regard for privacy. Naturally, the data on the Spirits was full of gaps, however.

That wasn't all. Shido had asked Reine for all the videos of the suspects and looked those over, as well. He knew that Ratatoskr had previously checked them over, but he had to see the tapes for himself.

"Already morning…huh?" Rubbing bleary eyes, he tapped at the computer and brought up the list of the remaining suspects.

Two days since Tohka disappeared.

During that time, Shido had failed to identify the culprit twice, and a total of four suspects had disappeared.

The day after Tohka vanished, Tama, named by Shido, and Tonomachi had disappeared. The next day, Shido had gone back to the beginning to reconsider all the information and named Mai Hazakura, who like Tama hadn't mentioned any past details, and then Mai and Mii vanished.

Only Kotori, Origami, Kaguya, and Miku were left now. But no matter how much he looked into these four, he could find no sign that any of them was Natsumi.

"…"

Shido forced the gears of his hazy mind to turn. There was something he kept tripping over.

Suspects who seemed firmly in the clear. This fact had caused a single possibility to sprout in the back of his mind.

He still had no proof. And it wasn't like he knew for sure who Natsumi had turned into. But this possibility was a thought was like a powerful poison that could upend everything he'd done so far.

"What is this…?" He put a hand to his mouth, elbows propped up on his desk. Maybe it was because of a lack of sleep or because of the excessive stress; just this movement roused some nausea.

He fell into silent contemplation, and the door behind him opened abruptly.

"Shido." Kotori stepped inside and frowned. "Hey. Whoa. Have you been up all night?"

"...Hey, Kotori."

"I told you not to push yourself too hard," she said, sternly. "I get how you feel, but all of this'll be for nothing if you collapse, you know?!"

"I'm fine missing a night of sleep. Today... I'm reviewing everything from the ground up today. Umm, first up is Kaguya?" Shido replied, eyes half-closed, and he reached out to pick up a document that had fallen on the floor. But he was struck with a sudden dizziness and fell to his knees. "Ungh..."

"Aaah, come on. I *told* you!" Kotori said, irritated, and took his hand. "Seriously! You have to rest right now. You're in no shape to make any kind of decision!"

"I don't...have time for that," he mumbled. "I'm *this* close to figuring it out. I have to hurry and find Natsumi."

"Not right now you don't. I was planning on canceling the investigation today, anyway, so just get some sleep."

"...!"

Shido brushed her hand away. "Cancel? What do you mean? Then I'll have even fewer clues, though? Why would you...?!"

"Just calm down." Kotori brought a chopping hand down on Shido's head.

It wasn't as though she had put any real power into it, but for Shido in his current state, it was a fierce blow. He fell forward at the brain-shaking impact.

"Ngh," he groaned.

"Just stay there and look at this." Kotori showed him the white card in her hand.

For a second, he thought it was the message from Natsumi that had come with the photos, but it seemed that the text was different. He blinked and read the words on the card.

"How about we bring our game to an end?
Catch me tonight.
Otherwise, everyone *disappears.*
Natsumi"

"Wha…" Shido gasped, as he sat up and took the card from Kotori's hand. "What…on earth."

"It was in the postbox when I woke up this morning," Kotori told him. "A challenge from Natsumi…I guess."

He swallowed hard. "Tonight… If I don't find Natsumi, the remaining suspects will all disappear. Is that it?"

"If we take this card at face value, then yes, that's it." Kotori shrugged.

Shido pressed a hand to his forehead. He'd done what he could. He'd looked into everything he could think of. But even so, he still couldn't pick Natsumi out of the four remaining suspects.

But…the end of his time had come so abruptly, the idea of not panicking was absurd.

If he got it wrong that day, the remaining suspects would all be taken. This overwhelming pressure made it hard to breathe.

But Shido clenched his jaw. "Kotori. I need a favor. Hear me out?"

"What? I'll do what I can," Kotori replied, quietly.

Shido slowly outlined his proposal, pulling his thoughts together as he went.

A few minutes later, Kotori put a hand to her chin, thoughtfully. "Makes sense. Okay. I'll make the arrangements."

"Thanks," he said. "To be honest, I'm still short of a full hand, though."

"Anyway, until we do this, you are getting some sleep," Kotori said. "That's my condition for helping."

"Okay. Got it." Shido nodded, obediently, stood up, and staggered over to his bed. He slowly raised a hand, bent his fingers down one after the other, and made a fist.

He still had no evidence of who Natsumi was impersonating. If this was a puzzle, the last few pieces had gotten lost somewhere. So he might have made the same request of Kotori regardless of whether or not he had gotten this challenge from Natsumi.

"Natsumi," he murmured, staring into space. "Tonight...I *will* find you."

"Hee-hee-hee... Hee-hee-hee!" Transformed into XXX, Natsumi giggled, quite pleased.

She remembered the look on Shido's face when Yuzuru disappeared the first night, Yoshino and Ai on the second, Tohka on the third, Tamae and Tonomachi on the fourth, and Mai and Mii on the fifth night. Fear and frustration and confusion and despair all mixed together, an indescribable expression. Each time she pictured it in the back of her mind, something akin to ecstasy ran through her.

But it was no good. It wasn't *enough*.

Natsumi craved more. A much greater terror than anything so far. Shido's face tortured with the ultimate despair.

Which was why she had sent one more note, a final letter to Shido. To erase all the suspects left. And to see his face in that moment.

And then when it was all over, to swallow up even Shido, forced to his knees by the unbearable loss.

"No one who's seen my secret can be allowed to go on. It's not enough to simply erase him. You'll live in pain after losing all of your friends," Natsumi said, and gritted her teeth. "After all...no one's ever going to come find me, anyway."

◇

That night, having gotten plenty of sleep (or rather, having been forced to get it), Shido was in a dim room with Kotori.

It was apparently part of an underground facility that belonged to Ratatoskr, but he didn't know the details. They'd had to walk a fair

ways from the entrance, so even the approximate area above ground was a complete mystery to him. The room was maybe thirty square meters. There were tall tables placed all over, but there was nothing else in the dance hall-like space.

It would have been more convenient if they'd been able to use the conference room on *Fraxinus* but given that one of the suspects was Origami and another was a disguised Natsumi, a Spirit whose power had not been sealed, they couldn't risk that.

Soon enough, he heard the sound of the door opening. And then three girls came inside on slow feet.

"Keh-keh! Is this not most suitable then! An appropriate stage for me to pass judgement over the distant king of the underworld!" The first was Kaguya.

"Woooow! It's like a secret baaase!" The second was Miku.

"..." And last was Origami.

Five people, including Shido and Kotori. All of the remaining suspects were gathered together here.

This was the favor Shido had asked of Kotori.

He wanted her to give him a place where he could bring all of the suspects together and talk to them. This was absolutely essential for him to shore up his conviction.

And there was one more thing. He honestly wanted to hear their thoughts as they came to the situation with fresh eyes.

Ratatoskr staff had already explained everything to them. Fortunately, he supposed, the people who were left knew about the existence of Spirits, so this was a hand he could play.

"Thanks for coming," Kotori said.

The girls walked over to Shido and Kotori, seeming somewhat perplexed.

Shido took a deep breath and looked at each of them in turn. "I know you've all heard what's going on. So first...let me apologize. I'm sorry. You all got dragged into this because of me. I'm really sorry."

He bowed, deeply. And heard them start to chatter.

"Hmph. Not a matter for concern. Indeed, given the severity of the issue, I would almost ask that you apologize for keeping silent."

"Mm-hmmm. So then that daaaate was part of your investigation? That's kind of too bad."

"…"

Shido bowed once more and then slowly lifted his face. "I know this is selfish of me. But please. I need your help!"

All the girls nodded, firmly. Except for one.

"Shido." Origami at last broke her silence as she stared hard at him. "What exactly is this?"

"Sorry. Origami. But please. I need you on board, too," Shido pleaded.

Origami lowered her eyes and shook her head. "I don't want you to get the wrong idea. I would naturally offer you my help. Especially if it involves Spirits. That's not what I'm asking about."

"Huh? Then…" He furrowed his brow.

"Where is this place?" she asked. "Who was it that explained the situation to us? I've wondered about this for a while. What kind of connections do you have, exactly?"

"Th-that's…" Shido stammered. These were in fact natural questions from Origami's perspective.

"If you worry too much about the little things, you'll get wrinkles," Kotori said, from where she stood to the left of Shido.

Origami turned a thorny stare on Kotori. "Kotori Itsuka."

"…What," Kotori replied, half-rolling her eyes.

For a moment, the two of them stared at each other.

Now that he thought about it, they had a history together. Origami had once suspected Kotori of killing her parents and attacked her for revenge. In the end, she learned that this was a misunderstanding, and it had been Shido who stood between them and kept them from fighting, but that hadn't erased the delicate connection they shared.

Origami lowered her gaze and sighed. "Tell me the story later. For the time being, I have no objection to cooperating with Shido."

"O-okay," he stammered. "Thanks, Origami."

"It's fine. But."

"But?"

"You asked me out so suddenly, I had gotten my hopes up a little."

"…That's… Well, uh, I'm sorry."

That was all he could say. He bowed his head. In fact, it had been Reine who contacted Origami and the others to bring them here, so he had no idea what kind of invitation they'd received.

"Keh-keh! It appears the issue has been resolved." Kaguya threw her hands out to strike a pose. "In which case, shall we not begin? The ritual of selection to smoke out the traitor lurking in our midst!"

"Goodness! You're full of fire, hmm?" Kotori remarked.

"Is that not only natural?!" Kaguya spread her hands dramatically. "The villain who absconded with Yuzuru is here among us, yes? Then we must find her and deal the appropriate punishment. I'll lose it otherwise!"

Her true voice slipped out toward the end. Kaguya cleared her throat and posed anew.

"At any rate! We shall unearth this Spirit or what have you that has erased Yuzuru and the others!"

She made a fist. It was an unusual way of showing strength. She was no doubt directing all her suppressed emotions since Yuzuru's sudden disappearance toward the culprit behind it all.

"Yeah, yeah. I get that you're raring to go, so just calm yourself for the time being." Kotori flicked the stick of the Chupa Chups in her mouth. "The situation is exactly as you were told before arriving here. One of us is a Spirit with the power of transformation, and we have to find her. The results of the investigation thus far have been summed up in these documents. No question or concern is too small. Speak freely."

She waved toward a nearby table where multiple sets of papers fastened with binder clips sat.

Everyone picked up a set and spent a few minutes looking over the documents.

Before too long, Miku let out a sigh. "I seeee. So that's what you meant with your question that time, darling."

"Darling?" Origami's eyebrows twitched.

Shido hurriedly spoke up. "W-well, how about we deal with that later?"

"…"

Origami looked unhappy, but she said nothing and dropped her gaze to the papers once more.

"Shido," Kaguya said. "What appearance does this Natsumi, or what have you, take on exactly?"

"Huh? Oh, that's—"

"She's hideous, terrifying to look at." Kotori cut Shido off. "Her face is like a toad that got hit by a car. Bulging eyes too far apart, piggy little nose, skin covered in pockmarks like moon craters. She's pretty tubby, too. No shape at all—bust, waist, and hips basically all the same size. And her face is just huge. Like her head's half her body. She's less Spirit and more monster, y'know?"

She rattled off this description of Natsumi with a straight face. But this very much did not match up with the Natsumi in Shido's memory; it was clearly complete nonsense.

"Hey, Kotori," Shido started.

Kotori put a finger to her lips. "Shh!"

And that's when he understood. She was trying to get a reaction out of Natsumi. There weren't too many people who would take it entirely in stride if they were described in such an unflattering way. Even if it didn't show up in her face or actions, there might have been some kind of reaction in the measurement devices set up in the room.

However.

"…*No reactions we can see.*"

Shido heard Reine's voice in his right ear.

Kotori had likely received the same report. *Tch!* She clicked her tongue and tapped at a small terminal on the table.

"Gotta be kidding me. Take a look," Kotori said, and Natsumi popped up on her screen. She was a beautiful woman in a witchy Astral Dress.

"Whaaat? She doesn't look at all how you said. You're quite the scary girl, Kotori." Miku said, perturbed.

But Kotori paid her no mind and pushed with a question. "You got anything?"

"It is somewhat concerning that you and Shido have been unable to grasp the tail of this beast after all this." The next to speak was Kaguya. "To start, is it indeed a certainty that this Natsumi or what have you is among us? Is there not the possibility that this transformation business was a lie, and she merely wishes to watch Shido panic and soak in that joy?"

"Naturally, that possibility exists. However..." Kotori crossed her arms and signaled Shido with her eyes.

Shido nodded in response. "Yeah. I didn't get to talk to her for very long. But I don't think she's the type to lie."

"Oh-ho?" Kaguya raised an eyebrow. "And how is it you can say that? This is the Spirit who removed Yuzuru and many others, yes? To trust her would be difficult."

"Mm. I don't know, it's like," he paused, briefly. "I felt like Natsumi's super confident in her abilities. And she declared that she was in the pictures. She might bend the rules, but I don't think she'd actually break them so obviously."

"Mm-hmm." Kaguya frowned and then nodded to indicate her acceptance of this. "I see then. Well, you are the one who has spoken with Natsumi directly. Worthy of trust, I should say."

Soon after, Origami lifted her face, apparently done reading all the papers. "Shido. Is it possible to see the photos and cards that Witch sent?"

"Yeah, sure," Shido agreed. He pulled a white envelope out of his bag and handed it to Origami.

"..."

Origami lined up the photos and cards on the table, while Kaguya and Miku peeked at them from either side of her.

"Mm-hmm. Indeed." Kaguya snorted. "The photos were taken without our knowledge then."

"Aah! My eyes are half-cloooosed!" Miku was indignant.

But Origami ignored them and moved her gaze over the photos and cards. She put a hand to her chin and was silent for a while before raising her face at last.

"There's one thing I'd like to confirm."

"Yeah? What?" Shido asked.

"The Witch's transformation abilities," she said. "Is it possible for her to transform into something other than a human being or a Spirit?"

"Huh?" His eyes grew wide in surprise. "Something other than a human being or a Spirit?"

"Yes." She nodded. "To be more precise, is it possible for her to transform into a substance with no life signs or a being that is clearly a different mass than her original form? For instance, could she become small enough to fit in your hand or thin like a sheet of paper?"

Now that she mentioned it, when Shido first met Natsumi, she had transformed the AST members into funny characters. If she could do it to someone else, it wouldn't be strange at all if she could transform herself into something other than a human being.

"It's probably possible," he said, finally. "But I don't know if she could turn into something of a radically different size, though."

"Meaning you can't definitively say it's impossible?" Origami pressed.

"Yeah…I guess not."

"Oh." She nodded.

Miku clapped her hands like she'd just thought of something. "Oh! So then maybe…" She pointed at the pictures on the table. "You mean maybe the Spirit turned into one of these piiiictures…or something like that?"

"Pictures…" Shido put a hand on his chin. True. He couldn't completely reject the idea.

"I'm in here. Can you guess who I am?"

Right. From that text on the card, "in here" could indeed have meant that Natsumi was inside a photograph itself.

"Yes." Origami glanced at Miku and nodded, firmly. "Normally, if you were shown a photograph and told 'I'm in here,' you would think the Spirit was inside of the person in the photograph. But in this case, she did not specifically say that."

She glared at the photos as she continued.

"To start with, there's something off about the rule itself. The more time passes, the fewer suspects there are. It's true that this might be an effective means of instilling panic in Shido. But at the same time, it runs the risk of making it easier for him to find her. She wouldn't use such a method unless she was certain that he would never manage it."

Shido nodded. This was the same question he'd had.

"Indeed." Kaguya sniffed and crossed her arms. "But supposing that were so, how to proceed? There are twelve photos here. You mean to point the finger at each and every picture?"

"No need for that," Origami said, and pulled the pictures on the table together into a pile.

"Origami?" Shido said, doubtfully.

"Watch." She reached a hand into her pocket, and there was a *chak* sound. A knife plunged into the pile of photos. The blade went through all of them and stabbed into the table.

"Ee?!" he yelped.

"This is the simplest and quickest way to check," Origami told him, her expression perfectly blank, and twisted the knife in the stack.

But the photos did not react.

"It seems that was incorrect," she said, with a hint of regret in her voice, as she put the knife back into her pocket.

Shido wiped away the sweat on his forehead with one hand. All the while wondering what would have happened to Natsumi if she really had transformed into a picture.

"Hmph." Kotori snorted. "Back to square one then?"

"Buuut I think Origami's right, though. This doesn't feel like Natsumi enjoying empty thriiiiills. I think she's bending the rules so that there's no way anyone will be able to guess the right answer. I mean, there are only four suspects left? Isn't there a real chaaaance that even if you take a shot in the dark, you might get a hit?" Miku said, placing a finger on her chin thoughtfully.

Shido was entirely in agreement with her.

However. Kaguya looked at Miku with a complicated expression. "Meaning? Do you presume to say that Natsumi is not among the suspects? Did Shido not just reject this idea?"

"I-I wasn't saying that, buuut…"

"Or perhaps you wish to make us believe that Natsumi is not among us?" Kaguya said, narrowing her eyes.

Miku's mouth twisted downward into a pout. "What's thaaat supposed to mean? I will get mad at you, you know, Kaguya!"

"Hmph. Do you panic because my aim was true? You grow more suspicious. Your evil intentions are visible in the jet-black aura around you."

"Hey! Both of you! Settle down!" Kotori hurriedly got between Kaguya and Miku. The two girls glared at each other over her head for a moment. "This is not the time for picking fights. Shido, you tell them, too."

"…"

But Shido was silently looking at them with his hand covering his mouth.

"Shido?" Kotori said. "What's up?"

"Oh, actually, what if—" he muttered to himself and ran his fingers through his hair vigorously. "Origami, can I see those pictures a sec?"

"Okay." Origami handed him the bundle of knife-punctured pictures.

Shido laid them out in front of him and stared at them intently. "Four suspects left. But no matter how deep I dig, I can't find any hint of Natsumi among them. She's bending the rules so that I'll never be able to guess right. 'I'm in here. Can you guess who I am?'…"

He had come up with one possibility after days and nights of close examination of every bit of information he could get a hold of.

Muttering to himself, half-cursing, he exhaled at length. And then he let his gaze run over the others and spoke. "What if Natsumi isn't any of you?"

"Huh?"

All eyes grew round in surprise.

However, that was only natural. They had been brought together to find Natsumi, and now he was saying Natsumi might not have been among them. This was a bit like the cart before the horse.

"Hang on." Kotori frowned. "What are you saying, Shido?"

"Precisely." Kaguya nodded. "Is this not in direct contrast to your earlier words?"

But Shido shook his head. "No, I'm not saying that Natsumi isn't someone in the photos. At best, I'm saying she's not any of the four remaining suspects."

"…!"

Kotori's eyebrows jumped up a beat later; perhaps she had guessed at the implication of his words. And then she began to flip through the documents at hand at lightning speed.

Kaguya and Miku gaped at her.

"I get it." Kotori nodded to herself. "No way… But then…"

"Huh? What? Heeey, don't just talk to yourseeelf! Tell us!" Miku pestered Kotori.

She looked up, appearing almost feverish. "Yes. Maybe this—"

The twisting of a space in the middle of the room interrupted her, a faint glow spilling out of the spot, and the Angel Haniel appeared.

"Wha…?!"

The girls all cried out in confusion.

Shido hurriedly cast a glance at the clock. It was 11:30 PM, still half an hour left before midnight.

"What's this mean? Today's not over yet, though!" he shouted.

As if in response, the end of Haniel opened, and Natsumi popped up.

"*Hee-hee-hee! Don't panic, kid. It's our last night. You need to have more fun with this, okay?*" Smiling cheerfully, Natsumi continued. "*Special rule for the final night. I'll give you ten times the usual time to pick someone—ten whole minutes. If you don't guess who I am in ten minutes, or you don't guess at all, then I'll give you another ten minutes. If in the end, you haven't guessed right by the time there's one suspect left, then you lose. I will take the* existence *of everyone here for myself."*

"Ngh!" Shido grimaced, and he heard Kotori click her tongue.

"Thirty minutes…huh?" Kotori said, slowly. "You do think up some dirty tricks."

"Meaning?" Shido asked.

"Four remaining suspects," Origami said. Glaring at Natsumi, she continued, quietly. "If you go over the time limit without picking the culprit, then at exactly midnight, there will be one suspect left. In other words, the Witch will end the game at the same time as the date changes."

Shido clenched his hands into fists and looked at the girls in the room once more.

Kotori, Origami, Kaguya, Miku.

Their faces were all colored with tension and fear and frustration. Just looking at them, it seemed impossible that one of them could be a Spirit who was trying to steal everyone's "existence."

"Oh, right, right," Natsumi said, as if to interrupt Shido's train of thought. *"Since you've all gathered together here so thoughtfully, I don't mind if someone other than Shido guesses. But, of course, it's one guess every ten minutes, so think very hard before you speak. If the number of votes is the same, then I'll consider that guess void."*

"You really just do whatever you want." Shido scowled at the new rule she tacked on.

But he couldn't stand here confused forever. He had thirty minutes left. And just three more chances to guess who Natsumi was. If he guessed wrong now, everyone there would be taken by Haniel. He absolutely could not fail.

Kotori looked toward Natsumi reflected in Haniel's mirror. "Perfect timing. There's something I wanted to confirm with the gamemaster."

"Oh my! And what would that be?"

"The rules of this game are that you're in one of these pictures. One person disappears every day we don't guess who you are. If we name the wrong person, that person will also disappear... That's correct, right?"

Natsumi shrugged, jokingly. *"Who can say...is what I'd like to say. But well, I can answer you that much at least. Your understanding is not wrong."*

"Oh." Kotori shot a glance at Shido as she snorted a little.

He nodded in return. That was the very question he himself had been about to pose.

"Wh-what is the meaning of this? Oi, Kotori, explain yourself!" Kaguya said, brow furrowed.

Kotori dropped her papers on the table. "We may have seriously misunderstood things."

"What?" Kaguya tilted her head.

Kotori sifted through the photos lined up on the table. "We've been trying to find Natsumi among the people shown in these pictures."

"Mm-hmm." Kaguya nodded. "But is that not the rule of the game?"

"Right. There's no mistake about that premise. But what if our thinking was pushed in a certain direction?" As she spoke, Kotori separated the photos into two groups.

On the left were Origami, Kotori, Kaguya, and Miku. On the right were the other eight. Basically, the suspects still remaining and the people who had already disappeared.

"M-meaning?"

"That thing Tobiichi and Miku were talking about before's really been bugging me. The four of us were investigated and analyzed in greater detail than any of the others suspects. Of course, we're up against a Spirit, so it would be no surprise if she had power that exceeded our expectations. But if Natsumi's actually not one of us, then everything makes sense."

"Ngah?!"

"Whaaat?!"

"...!"

Kaguya and Miku cried out in surprise, but Origami began to flip through the documents she held, her eyes growing wide.

She let her gaze crawl over the text and then slowly lifted her face. "I see. It's true that it isn't written anywhere."

"W-wait just a second! You mean…" Miku said, pressing a hand to her forehead as if to try and bring peace to the chaos in her mind.

"Yes." Shido nodded, firmly. "It's natural to assume the culprit would be among the remaining suspects. But this isn't a mystery novel. The other suspects might have disappeared, but they aren't dead. Nowhere in the rules does it say that whoever disappears at the end of the day *isn't* Natsumi."

"…?!"

Kaguya and Miku both gasped together, eyes wide as saucers.

Yes. This was the lone possibility Shido had arrived at.

Four remaining suspects that he found no reason to question no matter how he dug into them. And a rule that would put Natsumi at a disadvantage as the game progressed.

If this theory was correct, then it linked everything together.

"Thus, Shido. Kotori. Do you mean to say that Natsumi is not among those gathered here but rather one of those who have vanished already?" Kaguya asked, nervously.

Kotori put a hand to her chin, a complicated look on her face. "Actually, it's more like of the people who have already disappeared, it's someone *other than* the people who disappeared because Shido named them. It would definitely be against the rules for her to lie when Shido guessed correctly."

She pulled the pictures of Yoshino, Tama, and Mai out from the group on the right side, leaving five photos: Yuzuru, Ai, Tohka, Tonomachi, and Mii. These were the people Natsumi had taken at the end of each day.

"W-w-wait just a moooment!" Miku cried out. "Doesn't this make it moore difficult? Now we have more suspects!"

And indeed there were five of them now. Given that they only had three more guesses, the number of options was too large.

However.

Origami shook her head. "It looks that way in terms of numbers.

But it's not actually more difficult. Looking through these papers, we can see there is just one person who would have guaranteed Natsumi's safety."

· "Huh?" Shido scrunched his eyebrows. The conclusion he had reached was just the Natsumi candidates; he still had no decisive proof that narrowed them down to one.

But Kotori nodded in agreement with Origami. "Yes. If a suspect were to disappear before they could be named, then they would vanish from our minds as a possibility. Making that person a sure bet for Natsumi."

Eyebrows rising, she continued.

"But even if that is the case, the initial conditions were the same for everyone. No matter how low the probability, if Shido named her before she disappeared, then Natsumi would lose. Shido, think. There was just one person. One person who didn't rely on coincidence to escape potentially being named by you."

Shido racked his brain and quickly hit upon the person Kotori and Origami were talking about.

"No way... Yuzuru...?" He spoke the name of the girl who disappeared the first night and swallowed hard. Kotori and Origami looked away, indicating their agreement.

But Yuzuru's sister Kaguya scowled with displeasure.

"What say you? Do you mean to say Yuzuru is the culprit?" She brought her face in close, and Shido hurriedly shook his head.

"Wait. Stop. I wasn't—"

But Kotori cut him off. "It's in the documents. Haniel only started to show up and push Shido to name someone on the second night."

It was exactly as she said. Haniel hadn't appeared on the first night. In other words, Shido hadn't been given a way to guess who Natsumi was. And that night, Yuzuru had been taken. At the time, he had trembled in fear at the fact that a suspect disappeared, but when he thought about it now, he didn't understand why Haniel hadn't shown up on the first day.

"The first night. Yuzuru was taken," Kotori added. "To put it another way, doesn't that mean Shido would definitely not guess it was her after that?"

Kaguya looked sick at the fact that Yuzuru was under suspicion, but perhaps unable to find any ammunition to argue it, she pursed her lips shut.

Kotori sighed and turned toward Natsumi. "Such a mean little idea. But as a result, your meticulous caution actually gave us something on you. The person you're impersonating is Yuzuru," she said, confidently.

"…"

Shido sank into deep thought. This *did* make sense. But for some reason, he couldn't help feeling that there was still some decisive something missing.

"*Hmph. You're sure about that?*" Natsumi replied, leisurely. "*That's exactly ten minutes. Everyone in agreement with Kotori, please raise your hands.*"

Kotori, Origami, Miku, and Kaguya—reluctantly—raised their hands.

The corners of Natsumi's mouth turned up in Haniel's mirror. "*Okay, that's time up. A majority vote has selected Yuzuru Yamai.*" She snapped her fingers.

"Wha—"

Origami glowed faintly and was sucked into Haniel's mirror.

"O-Origami?!"

"*Hee hee! Try. A…gain! Your thought process was interesting, but tooooo baaaad!*" Natsumi laughed, as if it was all too hilarious, and whirled a finger around like she was issuing a challenge to Shido and the remaining girls. "*Well, the person you named is Yuzuru, and she's already gone, so I can only erase one person, unfortunately. Hee hee! Two chances left. I wonder if you'll be able to guess right?*"

"I-impossible." A shiver of fear ran across Kotori's face. "You're saying it wasn't Yuzuru?! Th-then who exactly…?!" She set her elbows on the table and cradled her head in her hands.

And of course she did. At the eleventh hour, they were back at square one. There was no time before their next guess. The tension was so great, their hearts practically leaped out of their chests.

"Ngh…" Shido turned toward the documents once again.

Yuzuru was not Natsumi. So then was it one of the people left in that group—Tohka, Ai, Tonomachi, Mii? But no one other than Yuzuru had any guarantee that they wouldn't have been selected by Shido. Had Natsumi actually opened herself up to danger simply for the sake of having fun with the game?

But if he let his thoughts go in that direction, then that very premise was meaningless. If Natsumi was just having fun, she could easily have been one of the three remaining suspects. Or…

Thoughts raced through his mind, and he pressed his index fingers up against his temples as if to try and bring peace to his brain.

"*Hee hee! Ha-ha-ha-ha-ha!*" Natsumi burst out laughing, clutching her stomach, as if delighting in their confusion. "*My, my, it's rough, hmm? Are you done playing detective? If you don't hurry up and find me, you'll all be chumming it up in the mirror world, you know? Hee hee! But don't worry. I'll make good use of all of your appearances.*"

"This…wretch!" Kaguya kicked at the floor and charged toward Haniel. "How dare you take Yuzuru! Tohka! Yoshino! Origami! Tama! Ai, Mai, Mii! And Shido's friend! Give them back! Give them back!!"

But there was no way such an attack would work on an Angel. Haniel shone hazily, and Kaguya was easily sent flying.

"Ngah!" She groaned when she slammed into the wall.

"Kaguya!"

"You're wasting your time! Stop! Even if you could use your limited Spirit powers, you don't have the strength to take on an Angel the way you are now," Kotori said, a stern look on her face.

"S-so we should just leave it?!" Kaguya clenched her hands into fists and was about to take another swing at Haniel when Natsumi spoke again.

"*You've been running around doing this and that, but the time's come. It seems you haven't picked anyone yet. What's it going to be?*"

Before they knew it, ten minutes had gone by.

"I guess you don't have a pick, hmm? In that case—" Natsumi started to say.

"Tohka!" Kotori shouted.

"K-Kotori?" Shido stared at her. "You're saying Tohka is Natsumi?"

"…To be honest, it's a stab in the dark," she replied. "But we can't waste a valuable chance to guess."

"So it's Tohka then?" Natsumi asked.

Shido couldn't think of anyone, either. Begrudgingly, he nodded his assent.

This time, Kaguya shone faintly and was sucked into the Angel.

"Wh-whoa!"

"Kaguya!"

"Too bad. Tohka's a miss, too. And midnight's in ten minutes. Your next pick's your last chance. Hee hee! Now, I wonder if you can guess who I am?"

And then silence fell over the room once more.

But that didn't last long. Miku began to shout, head in her hands.

"Wh-what is going on?! I haaaate this! Please let me go hooooome!"

"Calm down!" Shido cried. "You have to calm down, Miku! Getting upset is playing right into Natsumi's hands!"

"D-darling… It's just, I mean…!" Tears filled her eyes, and she began to sob.

Shido gritted his teeth as he comforted her.

Something. He was missing something decisive. Natsumi being one of the people disappeared by Haniel… That had to be right. But he still didn't know who it was.

"Right. There's something, there has to be something." Kotori flipped frantically through the papers, sweat pouring down her forehead. "This snake woman wouldn't come to a fight empty-handed. There *has* to be something that would put her completely in the safe zone!"

Shido looked at the photos on the table. At the three people Natsumi had taken who had also not yet been picked by him.

But was Natsumi really one of them? He wasn't even sure of that anymore. He pressed a hand to his chest as if to try and settle his steadily increasing heart rate, as he looked back and forth between the papers and the pictures.

But no matter how hard he thought about it, an answer was not forthcoming.

"Sorry to disturb you in the middle of your struggles, but that's five minutes," Natsumi said, giggling.

Shido gasped. When he looked at the clock, he saw that five minutes had indeed gone by. Time had flown as he panicked. His fear elicited confusion, and confusion destroyed his judgment. With a shaky breath, he scratched madly at his head.

"Aaaaaaaah! Enough! I haaaate this!" Miku screamed, shoving her hands into her hair, unable to withstand the extreme tension. "Daaarling… I… I-I…!"

Her teeth began to chatter, and she pulled an ornament out of her hair and pushed it into Shido's hand.

"M-Miku? What—"

"I-if I disappear, too, please don't forget me! Look at this ornament and r-remember me," she pleaded.

"Don't talk like that! I'm not letting you disappear! I'm definitely going to find Natsumi!" he shouted and handed the hair ornament back to Miku. But she refused to take it. "Miku…?"

I-it's just… If I have it on me, won't it just disappeaaaar with me?!" she cried. "I-I can't bear to leave you with nothing of mine, darling!"

"What—"

And then.

"—"

Shido felt something like an electric current jolt him.

Origami was gone, Kaguya was gone. Only Kotori and Miku were left. And the timer was counting down. In a few minutes, Haniel would erase the final person. The situation was the definition of despair. This would normally be the time when resignation crept across a person's face. But Shido was shivering at the possibility that had flitted into his head.

The hole that he'd found in the rules: it wasn't necessarily the case that Natsumi was not one of the people who had already disappeared. And the words Miku had spoken just now: If she had it on her, it would disappear with her.

These two things connected with that annoying fog hanging over his head, that nagging feeling that something was off, and everything snapped into place.

"What if..." he started, half-dazed.

"Shido...?"

"D-darling?"

Kotori and Miku both turned dubious faces his way.

But he couldn't afford to respond. He simply stood on the spot and furiously pieced together information in his mind.

Now that he was thinking about it, this game had been strange right from the get-go. All he'd been given in the beginning were a couple of sentences. But over the days that followed, various elements had been added in. Based on these, which grew in number with each passing day, Shido, Kotori, and Reine had guessed at the rules Natsumi put in place. They'd been eager to try and grasp the true nature of this game.

That. What if *that* had been Natsumi's objective. What if the addition of these rules, which seemed like nothing more than caprice at first glance, were to hide a single phenomenon?

"'I'm in here. Can you guess who I am'..." Murmuring the rule that he'd spoken countless times, Shido dropped his gaze to one of the photos on the table. To a single point he had completely overlooked until that very moment. To a single photo that was clearly different from the other eleven.

"Natsumi. There's one thing I want to confirm," he said, turning his gaze toward the Spirit in the mirror.

"Hmm? What is it then? If you're going to beg for your life, I'm not interested, though," Natsumi replied, with a leisurely ease.

But Shido ignored that challenge and continued. "You sent me twelve photos. But are there really *twelve* suspects?"

Natsumi still showed no signs of being flustered in her reply. *"Hee hee! Well now, who can say?"*

But that was enough for Shido to be certain. Because she had answered Kotori's question earlier. And yet she dodged his now. Which was proof to back up his guess.

Shido recalled the conversation he'd had with this suspect a few days earlier.

"Ah..." A detail he hadn't paid particular attention to at the time came back to life in his mind.

There was no mistake.

Shido swallowed to wet his dry throat and slowly lifted his face. "I know. Kotori. Miku."

""...?!""

Kotori and Miku gasped. Natsumi raised an eyebrow.

"Y-you know?" Kotori said. "You mean, who Natsumi is?"

"R-really, daaarling?" Miku's face lit up.

"Yeah. Thanks to all of you." he replied. "I never would have figured it out alone."

"Who exactly is it, then?" Kotori asked, a dubious look on her face.

Shido took a deep breath and continued. "Our premise was wrong. Natsumi didn't move herself to the safe zone at the start of the game. She was *always* in the safe zone."

"What do you mean?" Kotori said.

"Natsumi's answer just now clinched it for me," he told her. "She never once said that there were *twelve* suspects."

"What...?" Miku's eyes grew round, and she began to count the photos on the table. But of course, there were still only twelve of them.

Shido slowly shook his head. "Yes, there *are* only twelve photos. But it wasn't Natsumi who defined the number of suspects; it was us. There were actually thirteen suspects—actually, it's more like twelve people and one *being*!"

"...!"

Kotori's eyebrows shot up her forehead. And she turned her eyes toward one of the photos. "I can't believe it. But it's true that if that's the case…"

"Darling, we're out of time! There's only thirty seconds left!" Miku shrieked.

Shido took a deep breath and slowly raised his right hand. "Natsumi is…you."

He pointed his index finger out toward Haniel.

"Isn't that right, *Yoshinon?!*"

Natsumi's reflection in Haniel looked back at Shido with a serious face, unlike the bold smile she'd been wearing thus far. "*Yoshinon, is it? I suppose you mean the puppet Yoshino carries around.*"

"Yeah, that's right." He nodded. "For these last few days, you've turned yourself into Yoshinon."

"*Perhaps you could clue me in on how you came to this conclusion,*" Natsumi asked, stroking her chin with one hand.

"I realized it thanks to Origami and Miku," Shido said, staring into her emerald eyes. "First, the possibility that you could turn into something other than a person. And the fact that whatever the suspect had on them disappeared with them. Thinking about these two facts together, the only thing I could think of was Yoshinon."

"…"

Natsumi crossed her arms, no expression on her face. Shido ignored this and continued.

"And once I realized this possibility, I remembered something strange."

"Strange?" Kotori asked.

"Yeah." He nodded without taking his eyes off of Natsumi. "When Yoshino and Yoshinon came to the house in costume on the first day of the investigation, I was so surprised at Yoshinon poking its head in through the opening in the door that I threw my cell phone at it."

"Now that you mention it, I feel like I did watch a video of that."

"But Yoshinon neatly avoided it," he said. "Almost like it could see the phone coming. But Yoshino's eyes were *definitely* on the other side of the door."

"Ah…!" Kotori's eyes flew open in surprise.

Yes. Talking to Yoshinon on a daily basis, they tended to forget. But Yoshinon was a personality that manifested through the puppet only when Yoshino had it on her left hand. It was completely dependent on Yoshino to sense anything. It shouldn't have been able to dodge the phone.

"And one more thing," he continued. "When I chatted with them about the past, Yoshinon talked about when it was at Origami's house. And it's true that when Yoshino lost Yoshinon, I found it in Origami's house. But there's no way it could know that. Away from Yoshino, Yoshinon's just a puppet."

It was impossible for Yoshinon to have known it had been kept somewhere else.

But Natsumi had known. Maybe she'd gone through his memories when she turned into him. Or maybe when she was assessing people to decide who to become, she'd learned about Yoshinon from Origami's journal. He didn't know how, but she had had information that Yoshinon couldn't have known.

"You spoke. And you could've just left all the talking and moving to Yoshino! I don't know if you wanted to add some info and clear away any suspicion, or if you were overconfident and trying to give me a hint, but you went and talked!"

He thrust his finger out at Haniel once more.

"So, how about it, Natsumi! Are you Yoshinon?!"

"…*That's—*" Natsumi hesitated.

Haniel shuddered. As the shuddering grew in intensity, the mirror at the end began to crack. And then the mirror emitted a powerful glow, unlike the faint light it had shone with so far.

A dazzling light, like several large spotlights combined into one, filled the room. Shido automatically shielded his face with his hands.

"Ngh!"

"Wh-what is this…?!"

"Eeeaah!"

Soon, the shining subsided, and his light-seared eyes finally could see again.

Shido noticed several people lying on the floor, people who hadn't been there a second ago.

Yes. His friends, all the people disappeared by Haniel.

"You're back!!" Shido shouted, and several of them sat up slowly, holding their heads.

"Wh-what on earth…?"

"I'm…back?"

"…!"

Tohka, Kaguya, and Origami all blinked rapidly. In the next instant, Kaguya seemed to guess what had happened; she whirled her head around and ran over to Yuzuru, lying limp on the ground.

"Yuzuru! Yuzuru!" Kaguya shook her sister.

A few seconds later, Yuzuru coughed, weakly. "Hazy. Kagu…ya. You are as boisterous as ever."

"Yuzuru!" Tears streaming down her face, Kaguya embraced her. Yuzuru looked at her blankly for a second, but then quickly hugged her back.

Tama, Tonomachi, and Ai-Mai-Mii were still unconscious. From watching Tohka and Yuzuru wake up, he guessed that it might simply have been the difference in resistance to Spirit powers rather than the order they had been taken by Haniel.

"Thank goodness. You're all…okay…" Shido heaved an enormous sigh and slumped to the ground, spent.

Although he had been bold in his declaration of the culprit, the truth was his heart had been pounding so hard, it threatened to rip in half.

"Shido!" Tohka ran over to him. "Wh-what happened? Where are we?"

"…Hey."

But now that the tension had been released, Shido didn't have the extra energy to even give a real response to Tohka's questions. He smiled, weakly, and stroked her hair.

"Ngh…! What's wrong, Shido? Mmm…" She had a doubtful look on her face, but eventually, she made a happy noise, like she was enjoying the hair stroking.

Shido was somehow enjoying himself now and the tension left his face.

But then out of the corner of his eye, he spotted a certain silhouette.

"That's…!"

A girl was crouched on the floor just like everyone else. A girl wearing a big witch's hat.

"Natsumi!" He tensed up all over again and stood with Tohka's help. And then he walked slowly over to the girl in question.

Everyone else had apparently noticed where Shido was heading. Origami, Kotori, Miku, and the Yamai sisters moved to encircle Natsumi.

"That's my win. I'll accept your surrender," Shido said.

"…!"

Natsumi's shoulders jumped up, and she slowly lifted her face.

The second he saw Natsumi hidden behind the broad brim of her hat, Shido forgot his nerves and cried out, stunned, "Huh?!"

The reason was simple. The girl on the floor before him now was entirely different from the Natsumi in Shido's memory.

Small, slender body. Unhealthily pale skin, and a stooped back that made her small body look even smaller. Spindly brows, eyes that drooped morosely, no trace of that confident expression. Her hair alone was just barely the same color as that of the Natsumi in his mind, but it wasn't shiny and long. It was a bird's nest, untouched by brush or comb. A small girl utterly unlike the sexy Natsumi crouched there before him.

"You're…Natsumi…right?" Shido said, brow furrowed doubtfully.

She gasped, patted her face, and looked shocked.

"Ah. Ah. Aaaah?!" she cried out in despair, grabbed onto the brim of her hat, and curled into herself even further in an attempt to hide.

"What…on earth…?" Shido cocked his head curiously.

"I get it." Kotori snorted softly. "So when you met her before, Shido, she had changed her appearance with her Spirit power."

"Oh." Shido's eyes grew round.

"—!"

Natsumi screamed a voiceless cry and raised her right hand high, still hiding herself in her hat.

"Haniel!"

The Angel floating in the center of the table came over to nestle itself into Natsumi's hand. The cracked mirror began to repair itself automatically.

In the next instant, Natsumi's body flashed with light, and then she transformed into the adult woman Shido was familiar with. She turned hateful eyes on Shido and then everyone else around her.

"You know," she said, in an oppressive tone. "You know you know you know you know you know you know you know you know you know you know you know you know you know you know you know you know you know you know you know you knooooooooooow!"

She twisted about in a fit of rage.

"You've seen my secret…not once, but twice…! I-I-I-I can't let you get away with this. Never. None of you. You'll all paaaaaaaay!" she shrieked and brandished her broom. "Haniel!"

"Wha…?!"

The bristled end of the Angel shone once more, and the room was saturated in a dazzling light.

"Ngh…!" He unconsciously closed his eyes and screwed up his face.

The light died out in a few seconds. His eyes adjusted, and the room returned to its gloom.

However.

"Shido! Shido!" Tohka cried, her voice higher than usual.

Shido turned to look at her and froze.

"Shido, what is this? My body won't listen to me!" Tohka kicked and flailed, trailing oversized pajamas, looking to be around eight years old.

"Wh-what?!" he gasped.

But that wasn't the only weird thing.

When he looked around at everyone, all of them—except the

unconscious members of their group—had grown younger, just like Tohka.

"What...on earth...?" He furrowed his brow.

"Hee hee! Hee-hee-hee-hee-hee-hee!" Natsumi laughed, breezily, Haniel still held up in the air. "Take that! You can aaaallll stay tiny babies forever!"

Natsumi cackled, and then straddling Haniel, opened a hole in the roof, and flew off into the sky.

"St-stop! Natsumi! Natsumiii!" he shouted, but his cries only echoed emptily in the room.

To be continued.

Afterword

It's been a while! Koushi Tachibana here. Natsuuumi!

I'm bringing you *Date A Live, Vol. 8: Search Natsumi*. This time, the story structure might be a bit unusual for me. It's a guessing game with Natsumi, a Spirit with powers of transformation, impersonating someone in Shido's life, and Shido trying to figure out who she is.

That said, however, as one other concept, I wanted to give each of the increasing number of characters a chance to shine, and I do hope you could have a bit of fun with that, too.

I'll just say now that the name of the Spirit who makes her first appearance in this volume is Natsumi, even though it's spelled with the characters for "seven sins." Kurumi's stronghold as the solid leader in the world of strange name pronunciations is as solid as ever, but Natsumi's is also read quite differently from the usual readings. Ever since the subtitle was announced for this volume, I've been getting emails from my friends with strange name pronunciations including "Yoshigyu" for Miku's kanji characters. The absolute worst has to be "Mosuba." At first, I didn't understand the meaning, but after thinking about it for a few seconds, I realized that it was patterned after the menu of a certain fast-food shop. Now that I'm thinking about it, I feel like when Yamai came up, it was read as "Habomai." But I do not accept that the characters are hard to read, hard to pronounce, or any such rubbish. It is simply a more terrific stretch of an interpretation.

Now then, one announcement.

Date A Live is set to receive a new manga adaptation in *Monthly Shonen Ace*! Yaaah! Clap clap!

This will not consist of side stories, but rather the novel series starting with *Date A Live, Vol. 1: Dead-End Tohka*. Sekihiko Inui will be in charge of the art. This is an artist highly praised for cool portrayals of action, so please do look forward to this release!

This book was created through the efforts of a number of people: Illustrator Tsunako, my editor, the designer Kusano and everyone else involved in the publication of the book, all the book store clerks, and more. We managed to get the book out again without issue. Thank you so much!

The next volume, *Date A Live, Vol. 9* will be released in December. This volume comes out in September, so the pace is a little quicker than usual, and there will be a special version with a Blu-ray, so you'll miss out if you're late. I'm already excited.

All right, then. I pray we will meet again.

Koushi Tachibana
August 2013